Praise for *T*

'A bare, lyrical story of a Dublin c
among the very best of Irish books this year. It's not easy
to make writing seem this simple. Like all good stories,
it never judges itself, and so it remains open, charming,
dignified, even when the subject matter drifts towards the
harrowing. A really fine book, evocative of a
not-so-distant past'
Colum McCann

'*Tatty* is one of those novels that's easy to read, hard to get
out of your head and almost impossible to describe.'
Arminta Wallace, *The Irish Times*

'Christine Dwyer Hickey's fourth novel, *Tatty*, beautiful
and heartbreaking, confirms that her skills are perfected,
and her exceptional talent is far from exhausted. Such
is Hickey's power that, as a reader, you'll soon feel that
you have become the very necessary person for Tatty –
someone who knows everything about her, and longs to
protect her. . . . Tatty devastates in a way that only the
most unsentimental novels can.'
Sunday Independent

'*Tatty* is a book that will haunt you long after you've turned the last page. . . . The book is not without its lighter moments, and the humour is much needed. A heartbreaking account of a disturbed childhood that makes for compulsive reading.'
RTÉ

'Dwyer Hickey's mastery of the child's voice is spectacular.'
Edel Coffey, *Sunday Tribune*

'Christine Dwyer Hickey's marvelous novel … is a wonderful achievement.'
Vincent Banville, *Irish Examiner*

'Deceptively simple and impossible to put down, *Tatty* is a powerful, tragic tale of a disintegrating family that's sparse but very well-written. Messages floated up between the lines as much as the words spoke for themselves, so much so that tears were shed more than once.
A power-house of a book.'
BiblioFemme.com

Praise for Christine Dwyer Hickey

'Some of the finest writing of this century and the last.'
Irish Independent

'Page-turning originality.'
Nuala O'Faolain

Tatty

Tatty

CHRISTINE DWYER HICKEY

NEW ISLAND

TATTY
First published in 2004 by
New Island Books
16 Priory Hall Office Park
Stillorgan
County Dublin
Republic of Ireland
www.newisland.ie

This edition published in 2020.

Paperback ISBN: 978-1-84840-761-9
eBook ISBN: 978-1-84840-775-6

British Library Cataloguing in Publication Data. A CIP catalogue record for this book is available from the British Library.

Typeset by JVR Creative India
Cover image © Tetiana Maslovska / Shutterstock
Cover design by Anna Morrison, annamorrison.com
Printed on FSC paper by ScandBook

Dublin One City One Book is an initiative of Dublin UNESCO City of Literature and Dublin City Council.

DUBLIN UNESCO
City of Literature

New Island Books is a member of Publishing Ireland.

For Denis

Introduction by
Dermot Bolger

FOR A NOVELIST, NO VOICE IS HARDER TO CATCH than that of a child; no voice is more urgent in its desperation to make itself heard and make sense of the confusing perimeters of its world. In fiction, no voice is more haunting for the reader who yearns to reach out when confronted by a child's bewilderment and, in real life, no voice is often so easily and tragically overlooked. A child's voice can transfix us when steering a novel. It reveals the micro-universe of their family through the prism of a limited, skewed perspective, as they strain for a vocabulary to articulate emotional experiences they still lack sufficient maturity to process.

This is especially true for children of heavy drinkers who discover that the personalities and priorities of their parents can abruptly alter during an evening. They have parents who may not stop loving them and whom they will not stop loving and desperately wanting to believe in. But their parents can disappear into a mist of alcohol and later re-emerge, oblivious to the emotional damage caused to children who are forced to lie awake as inadvertent eavesdroppers on furious late-night rows. Rows that rage like tornados through rooms downstairs, before they finally abate, leaving only an impenetrable silence in their wake the following morning.

Since its inception in 2006, Dublin's One City One Book programme has become an important celebration of books that significantly advance our understanding of life in Ireland's capital. Certain choices seemed obvious in their public intent, like James Plunkett's great saga, *Strumpet City*, which chronicled the historically important events of the 1913 Lock Out. Christine Dwyer Hickey's *Tatty* is an equally important and inspired choice in how it chronicles lives which are not played out within the vortex of moments of seismic change. Instead it contains a child's mosaic of memories from the hidden life of a troubled family – events that occur without earshot of its narrator who is initially oblivious to their true consequences. Indeed the novel's warm humour stems from her unintentionally hilarious misreading of situations.

In the past such familial difficulties were rarely spoken about in Irish society, out of a desire to conform to the cult of domestic respectability. This cult of perceived respectability was as pervasive an influence on people's behaviour as any religious indoctrination in mid-twentieth-century Ireland. We may have wished to eventually attain the Kingdom of Heaven, but in the meantime our more fervent wish was to keep up the pretence that, if we refused to mention a problem, we could pretend it didn't exist.

Therefore *Tatty* is devastating in its forensic examination of a Dublin family falling apart under the strain of two parents with a deepening dependency on alcohol. The novel is all the more heartrending for its quiet simplicity of the thoughts of its narrator who – during ten chapters, each one covering a year in her life – ages from a three-year-old who knows nothing of life to becoming a thirteen-year-old who knows more than someone her age should need to know. Her voice subtly alters to mirror her changing perceptions of her disintegrating family and the havoc wrought by alcoholism and depression. Christine Dwyer Hickey brilliantly displays an uncanny ability to allow Tatty's child-voice to steadily mature with each passing year while remaining true to her quest to grasp what is happening and to let her story, and her family's story, be heard.

This mission to tell – without seeking permission to tell – is built into the nickname bestowed on her. Her real name is Catherine but just before her fifth birthday, after she innocently tells her mother about the places to which her father took her during a long day's drinking, her father calls her 'a big fat tell-taler'. This nickname is gradually shortened from 'Tell-tale-tattler' to 'Tatty'.

After *Tatty's* first publication by New Island in 2004, Joseph O'Connor noted that 'Along with Hugo Hamilton's *The Speckled People*, it inaugurated a radically new way of writing about Irish childhoods'. Each of these classic hybrid novel-memoirs marked a radical shift in tone by their authors, a raw power stemming from the wounded innocence of their bewildered young narrators. When I first read *Tatty*, it felt that it might not be a case of Christine Dwyer Hickey finding this unique poignant voice as the voice finding her and demanding to be heard. As Hickey said about the initial stages of writing this book: "I felt the rhythm of it. I heard the little girl's voice. I wrote a page, then I called my daughter, who was six at the time, and asked her to read it. It sounded grand."

That voice contains the unintended humour of a child naively blurting out secrets while trying to conceal them for her parents' sake, inventing fantasy friends to populate her isolation and spinning outrageous yarns to cover up a creeping shame that stems from a gradual understanding of what sets her family apart.

While terrible things happen in *Tatty*, they are not done by terrible people but by people who find it impossible to conform to the preordained roles Irish society has allotted for them. Tatty's parents are unique in their circumstances and eccentric in comparison to straight-laced neighbours. Yet they battle to try and fit into a society where a mother can exhaust herself fighting a losing battle to get an education for her child with intellectual disabilities; where it is taken for granted that men can drink expansively and extravagantly in public while women must drink secretly at home; where depression is an unspoken stigma lurking behind closed curtains on every street in Dublin and family secrets are meant to stay within families. What makes *Tatty* a modern classic is how readers from radically different circumstances will catch something of their own reflection in the restrained dignified tone of its narrator, in her need not just to grasp the truth but at times to also tell ludicrous lies to create a parallel imaginative world in which she can try to make sense of her life.

This novel superbly evokes the Dublin of the late 1960s and early 1970s: its streets, pubs, race tracks and bar-room banter; its private homes where class is delineated by whether the front room is called a 'living room', a 'parlour' or a 'lounge'; its tolerance of male drinking in an era when road safety campaigns urged drivers to skip the fifth pint or – if·they had already lost track of how much they had drunk – to only drink two more pints before driving. Yet few political events of this period impinge upon Tatty's preoccupations. Instead we see life through the prism of a child who can only focus on those pieces of the jigsaw of the wider world that help her make sense of the dark domestic interior she is trapped within.

As a period piece *Tatty* would be a stunningly evocative piece of fiction, both poignant and imbued with rich comedy. But tragically *Tatty* will always remain a contemporary and relevant novel for so long as alcoholism continues to ravage families, with the consequent hurt caused to children caught up in its wake, and for so long as the causes of depression remain not fully acknowledged. This makes *Tatty* a novel not only pertinent and significant in Dublin, but in every society where any child lies awake, trying to make sense of angry voices in a room below them, desperate to reconcile the two people whom they love, unable to understand these adult addictions that leave them vulnerable and scared and seeking answers to problems they cannot yet articulate.

Tatty doesn't mean 'tell-taler': it means 'truth-sayer'. The simplicity of Tatty's story disarms us with her wounded dignity; her humour and humanity; her ability to forgive, even when confronted by actions beyond her comprehension. The wounded innocence of her voice leaves behind a haunting echo that readers will not easily forget.

1964

Mam says the baby can't see properly, not yet. He can't even see his own hands or feet. See, there's this veil in front of his eyes that makes everything fuzzy, so he can see the shapes of us moving around and he can hear all our voices coming out of the shapes, but he doesn't really know who we are, not yet. Mam says that any day now the veil's going to get these tiny holes in it and that bit by bit the holes will get bigger, till there's no veil left at all.

When this happens he'll be able to see us: he'll be able to see himself. He'll look at us all and he'll know all our voices. Then we won't be shapes anymore. We'll be his family instead.

Today is the baby's christening day. He got a name. A name that means light. But it means something else as well: it means not hot and not cold. That can be good or that can be bad. Say if you want to make tea and the water is only lukewarm, then it's bad. But say if Deirdre's bath water is lukewarm then it's good. Because

Deirdre might scald herself if the water is too hot. She loves the curly steam and tries to grab it and hold it in her hands, so you can't take your eyes off her for a second, Mam says.

The priest poured water over the baby's head and then his name was Luke. He held the baby's head in one hand and the other hand tipped out the water. It fell over the back of the baby's head and squeezed through the priest's big white fingers. Then the baby's mouth went wide open all the way up to his forehead. He sucked in a huge breath and when he let it out again, you never heard such a roar in your life. It was even louder than Deirdre can go. It flooded the church right up to the ceiling. It made loads of echoes that splashed off the walls.

Nothing wrong with his lungs anyway, Uncle Bren said and the adults looked at each other with smiley eyes. When Deirdre screeches they look at the ground.

The baby was tired out after his roar. He fell asleep in Aunt Sal's arms on the way back from the church. That fella, she said, he has me two arms broke.

Now he's awake again, propped up in his cot so everyone can see his dress called a robe.

If you stick the heels of your hands into your eyes and press them in as hard as they go, when you take them away and squish up your eyes you can see like maybe the baby can see. There's loads of spots, orange and yellow, and puddles of colour and millions of stars. You wait till they fade and the room comes back and when you look into the cot again there's something different about him this time. As if he can see. Or nearly see anyway. He's all excited, squinting and blinking, his little tongue sticks in and out. His little fingers scrab the air like he's pulling away the last bit of veil, and his feet punch the end of his dress. And you can guess what it is that has him excited: he's looking at the hole getting bigger and bigger, and the room getting clearer, the way the telly does when you twist the knob and the interference melts away. Imagine the shock in his little heart when he finds out there's more to see than blobs and blurs and noises running around that don't belong any-where. You better tell Mam.

Mam, you say, the baby can see.

But Mam isn't here. Mam! Mam!

You run into the bedroom. No sign of Mam. Just empty coats plonked on the bed, and a roundy mouth putting on lipstick, and a woman's eyes over the mouth looking out at you through the mirror.

Where's Mam?

Urhhh?

My Mam?

Haven't a clue dear.

You can't find Mam anywhere so you come back to the living-room, and his eyes are like a camera moving around. Stopping on one thing: *blink.* Then moving off somewhere else: *blink.* Like he's filling up his head with photographs of the house. But the house isn't itself today. The house is strange with glasses from the pub and ashtrays from the pub and empty corners with no piles of washing and no newspa-pers shoved under the sofa. Suppose he thinks his house is always like this? With stuff on the table you're not allowed touch: trifle bowls and fancy plates, roundy roses squashed in a vase and billions of biscuits and little pink buns and a big white table-cloth that makes the table look like a cake.

And everywhere bottles: on top of the sideboard, in brown bags in the hall or in a crate behind the back door. Uncle Matt drinks from a bottle that's big and fat with a picture of a woodpecker on the front. It hisses and spits when he twists the knob off, then comes out lovely, red and all bubbly, like lemonade. But it doesn't smell like lemonade. It smells like sick.

A crowd of aunties sitting in a row or getting up sometimes to pass out the sandwiches.

A load of cousins milling around or stopping sometimes to tell tales on each other.

Men at the wall looking at their watches, filling slanty glasses with slanty bottles of stout.

A queue of people, bursting to go, outside the door of the toilet.

And visitors, visitors all over the place, and all the noise that visitors make, and all the smoke that visitors blow goes twirling up to the ceiling.

Dad, you say, I think – I think the baby can see.

Open the window, Dad says, flapping his hand at the fog of smoke. Go on open it quick before the poor baba chokes.

The window's too tight so you call Jeannie over and tell her that maybe the baby can see. One, two, three, you push the window open together and the fog of smoke stretches itself out and comes snuffling across the room.

You lean over the cot, shove your head in, so maybe he'll look at you this time. You call Brian over. He gets off Aunt Sal's lap, goes down on his hunkers and squeezes his fat cheeks into the bars of the cot. Then Jeannie's face comes in at the baby, shaking her curly hair. Oh you cutey little cutey, you fat little cutey, can you see me? I'm your sister. Yes I am. Yes I –

Get away from that cot, Aunt Sal says with her empty lap. Get away from that cot, before you turn it over. Get away, I said, NOW. Then she goes back to eating her sandwich.

When the men eat sandwiches they open their gobs wide and stuff them in. When the women eat sandwiches they pluck them with their fingers bit by bit.

It makes your hand look like a goose's head eating sandwiches that way; it makes your fingers look like the beak. Sometimes they lift the top slice and take a peep in case they don't like what's inside, then they close the bread over and even if they don't like what's inside they eat it up anyway.

Dad, I think – I think the baby can see.

But Dad's in the corner now talking to his friends looking at their watches and some of the uncles are looking at the aunties to see if they're looking back. Talking about leaving the house and going down to the pub. Mam will go mad. She kept on saying, all day yesterday, all the day before, You better not. You better not. Even think about going to the pub.

But Dad hates houses and he hates sitting down. Dad likes the pub. When you go on a visit, he says, No thanks, no tea for me. Then he nods his head at the man in the house. Are you right? he says. We'll leave the girls to their chat. And off they go.

Then it's dark on the way home in the back of the car. And in the front Dad says loads of long sentences and Mam must be tired after her chat because she says hardly anything at all.

And you can look at the windows in town full of bright, in shops or on top of big buses. And you can feel your face wobbling like jelly when the car goes out of town and over the cobblestones, and you can see all the dark houses on all the dark roads; then you can lie down and look at the orange street lights, pulling you home on a long orange string.

When you go to a birthday party, you get jelly and icecream, cake and chocolate Rice Krispie buns. You say, Thank you very much for the lovely party, then go home with everyone else. If it's your birthday party, you say, Thanks very much for coming to my party and for the lovely present and all. When everyone's gone you look at the presents again, say which is your favourite and which is your worst. You spread out the cards, read all the poems inside; you suck the icing off the end of the candles. Then you say thanks to Mam for the lovely party and help her to clean up the table.

But when the adults have a party it isn't the same. They go a bit funny. Sometimes they sing and that can be good. They laugh and clap and make noble calls: that means you have to sing if you're picked even if you don't want to. Mam and Dad are happy when there's singing going on. Mam knows loads of songs: the one about summertime, the one about diamonds, the one where she wants an old-fashioned millionaire. Mam is the best singer of all. She sings like someone off the pictures. Aunt June's the scariest with her voice all shaky and dry. Uncle Matt's funny doing his letting on he's a woman walk with Aunt Winnie's handbag. Then everyone says he's a scream. Dad doesn't sing but he makes loads of jokes. Everyone's happy and everyone claps. Then it's time to go home and Mam and Dad stop enjoying themselves again.

If the party is in your house then Dad just goes to bed and Mam stays up and finishes her drink and smokes on her own. Then the next day the house is all smelly and you have to open the windows and make sure you empty all the bottles down the sink before you put them in the brown bags outside the back door.

Sometimes there's no singing only talking, except it's not really talking it's shouting instead. They don't listen to each other, because they're only waiting on their turn to shout. They say the same things over and over. They talk about things that happened years ago. Then there might be a row. Everyone goes home at different times. If one of them goes home too early the people who are left behind always say something about them. You hear loads of stuff because they forget to send you out. They're too busy shouting so they don't notice anything. They never notice anything. Even now they don't notice that the baby can see.

1965

SHE'S NEARLY FIVE AND GETS LOST AT THE RACES.
One minute she's standing behind Dad under his
long brown raincoat, the next minute she's lost.

She's standing under his long brown raincoat
and it's like as if she's inside her own little tent.
She can hear everything that's going on outside
but can only see what's inside the tent. The lin-
ing is shiny, with bumps here and there from all
the stuff that fell through his raincoat pockets:
pointy pen, roundy pill-box, a couple of coins
that must have wiggled all the way down to the
hem. The bigger things stayed in his pockets:
newspaper, notebook, liver-salts tin. And there's
the big fat bookful of horses' names that you
always see him reading.

She can see the bulge of his binoculars on
the far side of the coat and can hear the little
badges rattling off the strap every time he moves
his arm. She can see the dark shape of him in his
suit, and can hear the people's feet running by,
in and out of the rain.

Dad tells her that when he gives her the nudge that means she has to grab a hold of his jacket because he's going to start running and she has to run out behind him. Like a circus horse, he says, do you know what I mean?

She doesn't, but likes the sound of it anyway and can't wait for Dad to get going.

She pulls her hands out of her mittens so she can keep a good hold of his jacket. Then dances her feet up and down so they're ready to run the minute he gives her the nudge. But the rain is too bad, he says. The rain is long and icy. So he changes his mind and says he'll have to leave her behind. He pulls his coat away, lifts her up and puts her down in a doorway near the men's smelly toilets.

You stay here, he says, till I get back. Do you hear me now? You're not to budge, not an inch.

He tugs her collar up around her ears, tells her to put her mittens back on, pulls her pixie-cap down over her forehead, then leaves her.

As soon as she stops seeing his long brown raincoat she goes out after him. But there are too many big bodies in the way and too many brown coats and the cold rain keeps smacking her on the face. So she comes back in and follows the heat into the bar.

When Dad comes back to the doorway there's no sign of her anywhere and then he's up the wall. He runs around everywhere pulling at people's sleeves. Did you see? Did you see? A little girl, this size … copper-colour hair, a fringe … ?

He keeps going on about the fringe even though you wouldn't be able to see it, because he's forgotten already about the pixie-cap, and that he's pulled it down over her forehead.

The voice from the sky calls out her name. The voice from the sky tells everyone her business – her age, her size, where she lives and what she is wearing: brown jacket, brown trousers, yellow jumper. Dad told the voice what to say; if it had been Mam the clothes would have been different.

It would have been: a biscuit-coloured sheepskin coat, chocolate-brown slacks, a mustard polo-neck sweater, a cream-coloured pixie-cap. Because that's the way Mam always talks about clothes, like you could eat them. But Mam doesn't go to the races. She stays at home with Deirdre and Jeannie and Brian and baby Luke. Because Jeannie might have an asthma attack and in anyway she doesn't like to ask anyone to mind Deirdre on account of her always screeching.

When Dad finds her, she's behind the counter sitting on a beer crate. She has one rosy cheek from the big heater beside her and she's sucking a bottle of fizzy orange through a straw. She has one hand on top of the heater and her mitten is flapping from the string in the sleeve of her jacket. Dad starts shouting that it could have gone on fire. Then he starts shouting at the barman. Did you not hear her name being announced? You stupid fucker, are you deaf?

Ah how could I – the noise in this place? And wasn't she grand in there, not a bother on her? Wasn't she warm at least?

You'd no business taking her like that.

He didn't take me, she says. I went in myself.

What did you do that for?

Because the rain kept smacking me on the face and I don't like the men's smelly toilets.

Then Dad starts laughing his head off. He lifts her up and sits her on the counter and all the men have to hear how he found her when she was lost. And she keeps on saying, I wasn't lost, I wasn't lost, I *wasn't*.

But no one can hear her because the bar is stuffed with big men's voices bashing around.

You better not tell your mother, Dad says. Or there'll be murder. Do you hear me now? You won't get me into trouble?

I won't.

Is that a big fat promise?

Yes Daddy.

Say it.

It's a big fat promise.

When he opens the front door she runs under his arm and comes shouting into the house. Mam! Mam! I wasn't lost. I wasn't. They said I was. But I wasn't lost, I *wasn't*. That was the start of how Tatty got her name. But it wasn't the day. It was a later day, when she was five and a bit. Another day when she got to go everywhere with Dad.

CR

When you go to work with Dad you get up when it's dark and you're not allowed talk in case you wake up the house and because Dad has to listen to the weatherman on the radio. Then you get into the car and it's the only car on the road for ages.

Dad calls for the men. The car stops outside all their houses and Dad lets you beep the horn. Jackie Mac's house is a huge big house, with loads of doors and a window every minute. His face pops up when he hears the horn beep; he's wearing a shirt and tie. Dad says that's because he sleeps in his clothes with the bed right up against the window so all he has to do is sit up and it looks like he's ready for work.

And that's so funny, thinking about Jackie Mac sleeping in his clothes, popping his head up to the window, she can't stop laughing. Dad says she's like an oul fish flopping around in there in the back seat. And that makes her laugh even more, nearly wetting her pants, and then Dad starts laughing as well.

Hey Dad?

What?

If you're the boss how come his house is much bigger than ours?

That's not a house, that's the flats.

What does that mean – the flats?

It means you're not the boss.

And first the car is full of space, then, one by one, the men plonk in and you get squashed up beside the window, or else you might have to sit on a lap.

The Pig Quigley's lap is nice and fat but Jackie Mac's is very skinny. He gets into the car like he's still asleep; when he drops his head back you can hear his soft little snores in your ear. Then the car is full with the smell of men and the smell of paint and the smell of soap and the oniony smell of all the men's lunches. And nobody talks except maybe Dad telling them all their jobs for the day, so there's nothing to hear only coughs and yawns, or matches scratching and long pulls of smoke going *Ahh-fffff* out through teeth.

Dad drives through the country dropping off men and picking up men and everything's black but then bit by bit you can see the day coming out back to front. Then Dad has to do his jobs. He drives in and out of different gates, up and down different yards. Knocking on doors, shaking hands; climbing up a ladder with his big measuring tape; standing under the factory stairs counting silver paint-drums that come rolling down the slide. And he bangs the door when he gets out and he bangs the door when he gets back in again. And he keeps on doing that: *bang! bang!* And then it's time to go to the pub.

When you go out with the men you go to the pub. You get hooshed up on the bar stool. You get to do things you're not supposed to tell Mam about. Sometimes you get a little pint of stout.

A pint for me, Dad says, and a little pint for my pal here.

It tastes like black buttermilk, sour and thick. It stings the tubes in the inside of your ears on the way down. But you drink it all up and go *Haaa* the way Dad does and wipe your mouth on the back of your hand. Then you say, I want to go to the toilet, even if you don't, and you get lifted down off the stool and the men forget all about you.

You can turn on all the taps; you can make the toilets have a race, running in and out flushing all the chains. You can open all the doors and slap them shut again; you can come back outside and crawl all over the long bouncy seats by the wall.

In some of the pubs you can find out where the pub-man's wife is and it's always in the kitchen. Sometimes the kitchen is up the dark stairs, the whole house up there with a living-room and a dining-room and all. One of them even has a piano on the landing. But sometimes it's down the cold yard past the jerky red chickens, or else it might be just in the back through the bar.

She likes when you have to go through the bar.

You can look at all the bottles squeezed into their shelves: orange-black-raspberry-lemon and the queues of glasses and mustard jars and the big cardboard box with the shuffly crisp bags inside. There's the bin where the barman throws all the cigarette ends and the squashed-up napkins and the fat from the ham. There's his mixed-up footprints all over the sawdust; silver bottletops; blobs of spilt stout. There's the low-down sink where he washes his glasses and the high-up box where he keeps all the bets. You can see all these things when you walk through the bar and when you get to the end you turn around to make sure you're going the right way. Then the barman says, Go on, don't be shy. Go on through, she won't mind.

And the next thing you're in the kitchen.

Then the pubman's wife might ask, Did you have your dinner? And you always, always say no.

Because you get funny dinners in other people's kitchens. Dinners that don't taste the same as Mam's. It might be the same stuff, but they match it a different way on the plate and that's why it just doesn't taste the same.

She got the heel of a roast heart stuffed in the middle, and another time a dippy egg and turnips cut up like chips. She got five Kimberly biscuits and tea in a mug after one dinner and that was a bit greedy, like eating two meals at one go. Because Mam only gives you two biscuits and only at teatime. Once she got white pudding and mashed potatoes and stuff out of a tin that looked like sick but was called Russian salad, and that was the funniest dinner of all.

The woman who makes you your dinner might ask you your business. And even though Mam always warns her, Don't be telling those nosy oulones all your business, sometimes she gets mixed up and forgets. And it's hard to know what you're allowed to tell or not, because one minute it's: *Tell the truth and shame the devil.* The next minute it's: *Ah what did you have to go and tell them that for? I could kill you stone dead.*

Mam says when someone asks you your business all you have to say is: I don't know. But the questions about your business are nearly always the same, like: Do you have a telly and how many bedrooms and brothers and sisters? And that would be too stupid not to know if you had a telly or not, or how many bedrooms, or brothers and sisters.

The woman with the Kimberly biscuits asked her different questions. The woman with the Kimberly biscuits asked, How is your mammy and is she still a real glampuss?

What's a glampuss?

Does she still wear beautiful clothes?

I don't know.

Well, is she still lovely and slim then?

Oh no. Her tummy's still a good bit fat after getting baby Luke.

Another one? My God, he didn't give her much of a break, did he?

The woman with the Kimberly biscuits had a telly in her kitchen and a man and a woman were having a row on the telly. The Kimberly woman said she knew Dad from before and he was a real heartbreaker and no one could believe it when he finally got married to a youngone like Mam. Then she started looking at the telly.

The woman on the telly was wearing a frilly pinny. She had her hand on her hip and kept shaking her finger at the man and every time she gave out to him again, people you couldn't see kept on laughing all over the place.

Does your mammy ever give out to your daddy? the Kimberly woman asked her.

I don't know, she said.

Like if he came home drunk would she give out stink to him?

Don't know.

Oh, isn't that great? Your mammy must be very easy going so – is she?

Emmm … ?

So your mammy and daddy never fight then – is that what you're tellin' me?

Do you mean like a boxing match?

No. Like a row, like that pair on the telly.

I don't know. I mightn't hear them if I was asleep, but I'd hear all the people laughing.

Ah no, the Kimberly woman said, there wouldn't be anyone laughing. That's not real, that's just the telly.

Oh? Well, I don't know because I mightn't hear them anyway. I mightn't hear them if they were shouting and calling each other names. I mightn't know if Mam was screaming and Dad was slamming doors. And then if

Mam was crying in the living-room on her own? Well, I mightn't know that.

Is that right now … ? the Kimberly woman said.

It made her feel kind of itchy, the Kimberly woman asking her about Mam and Dad. It made her feel kind of ashamed and afraid as well in case she might have said something by mistake and maybe now she'd get in big trouble with Mam.

So the next time a pubman's wife asked her business she didn't say, I don't know, she told fibs instead. She said they had three tellys and ten bedrooms and that Mam wore her wedding dress and a big hat when she was washing the dishes and sweeping the floor and that made the woman laugh all over the place and call her a hard nut.

Oh you're a real hard nut, the woman said, and started laughing again.

It was nice being able to make the woman laugh. It was nice, and it was much easier than telling the truth.

When you go out with the women, you go to the shops or else you go to a house on a visit. You might be allowed out to play if it's not raining. But if it is raining you have to behave yourself inside. If it's not a fussy person's house Mam might let you go into their living-room. If the telly has started yet, you can watch *I Dream of Jeannie*, or else *Jackanory*, or *Crackerjack* if it's a Friday. Sometimes the living-room is called a parlour, or else a sitting-room, or maybe a front-room instead. But if the house belongs to Mam's friend Alice then it's called a lounge.

Why does Alice call her living-room a lounge, she asked Dad, when it's not even a pub?

Because it might as bloodywell be, was what Dad said.

If the house belongs to a fussy person you have to stay where Mam can keep an eye on you, in case you might break something. So that means you have to stay with the women.

They stay in the kitchen; they sit at the table and smoke cigarettes and drink tea and give out stink about the men and that's a bit mean because the men never give out about them. The men never say anything about them at all.

They say, Ah sound man what'll you have? Or, How is the form? Or else they talk about horses and stuff out of the papers. Then they might send you out on a message.

The barman in Myo's gave her a packet of crisps called King crisps. He gave her the crisps because she went across the road to the bookies all on her own with a very important note in an envelope. She looked right, she looked left, she looked right again. She went up on her tippy-toes and stretched up her hand and the man in the bookies shop pulled the envelope in. Then he gave her the envelope back with little coloured tickets inside.

She looked right, she looked left, she looked right again. She pushed the big glass door in as hard as her arms would go. Then she was back in the pub. She said the crisps were the nicest thing she ever tasted and asked Dad if they could move to Castleknock so she could eat King crisps all the time. Dad said she'd have to wait till she was big and then she could find a rich husband and live on Millionaire's Row.

What's rich, Dad?

Loads of money.

What's millionaires?

Loads and loads of money. See that fella sitting down there? He's one.

I am in me arse, the fella sitting down there said.

But Dad must have made a mistake about the fella sitting down there, because he didn't even buy any drink. Only Dad did again. He took a big bunch out of his pocket, licked his thumb and pulled out a note. He pointed the note around at all the men's glasses and the barman blew out a big breath and said, Same again, I suppose? like he was fed up of only Dad buying all the drink.

The men said good luck to Dad. Then they looked up at the telly and started shouting at the horses.

She ate all the big crisps, she ate all the small ones, she stuck her finger into the corners, scooped up the crumbs and sucked them off the top of her finger. Then she turned the bag inside out and licked it all over. The men stopped shouting. There was quiet for a second. Then they all burst out shouting again. One of them clapped his hands, rubbed them together and did a little dance. Then he went, Ya-fucken-hoooo, and Dad said, Here you – do you mind? Do you mind watching your language in front of the child?

They won loads of money and said it was all down to her: she was a smasher, a lucky star, the best little runner they ever had. But they didn't send her back out again, the man who said ya-fucken-hoooo went out instead. And then she was raging because she would have loved another packet of King crisps.

What's wrong with you? Dad said. What's the puss for?

Nothin'.

Nuttin, nuttin, the big fat mutton? Dad said.

No, just nothin'.

I know what's wrong with her, the barman says, I know why she has that puss. She's trying to stop the clock, that's what it is. She wants time to stay still, so she doesn't ever have to go home again.

Don't we all? goes this man sitting beside Dad. And some of the men sort of laughed.

Then the barman goes to her, Ah I'm only coddin' you chicken, I'm only jokin'. Here, just wait'n you see what I have for you now.

And he climbed up on a stool to the shelf at the top; she could see his face through the mirror, all worried. First it looked like he was going to give her the little bird with the roundy belly that stood up on one leg and was able to dip his long orange beak into a glass, up and down, over and over, all on his own. But the barman's hand didn't stop on the bird. It moved on further and landed on the white horse instead. But when he came back down and put the horse in her hand she loved him, because he was smooth and heavy and stood still on a stage, and it didn't matter if he couldn't do anything on his own because he was so lovely.

The barman said she'd have to think of a name for her horse and mind it very carefully.

But someone might break him, she said.

Who might?

Just someone.

What someone?

I don't know, one of my big sisters might. But by accident only.

Ah you mean poor Deirdre? Poor Deirdre doesn't understand. Tell you what, why don't you hide him from her, put him up somewhere safe, that way she won't be able to touch him. And then when you're big enough, I bet you anything you like, your daddy will buy you a horse of your own.

That's right, Dad said. When she's ten she gets her own little pony.

Do I Dad? Really Dad?

Didn't I promise you?

Yes.

Well then?

Well then they went into town.

Dad brought her to the hotel where he used to live before he got married.

The tablecloth fell down to the ground and the knives and forks were very shiny. A man with a uniform put a big cushion under her bum so she could reach up to the table; then he tucked a big napkin under her chin. But that made her look like a baby so Dad said she could put the napkin on her lap instead. Then the man in the uniform said, Oh I do beg your pardon mam. And that was a bit silly, calling her Mam, because she wasn't Mam. Mam was at home minding the house and minding Deirdre and minding Jeannie and minding Brian and minding baby Luke and minding the phone for Dad's messages. And making the dinner as well.

Then all the women came over with little white pinnys on them and little white caps and shook Dad's hand and one of them called Lal with a brown creasey face cried when she saw him and gave him a big sloppy kiss.

Don't tell your mother, he said, she might be jealous.

But Mam was much nicer looking than Lal and Mam had no brown creases on her face.

Then Lal started fussing at the stuff on the table, Dad's knife and fork, his pint of stout, moving them around then putting them back in the same place again.

So now, Lal said, tell us – is she lookin' after you all right?

Dad shook his head slow and made his face pretend sad, then he pulled back his jacket to show Lal his nobutton shirt sleeve.

Oh God isn't that only desperate! she said

Then he pulled his tie down to show her his nobutton collar.

Oh God, isn't that a disgrace! Do you know what it is? You should never have leavin' me. Tell you what. I still have me boxa buttons upstairs, if you want to go up and slip the shirt off for me.

And Dad goes, Lal! Might I remind you, I am now a married man.

Then Lal started laughing and clapping her hands, Oh you're still the same divil, the very same divil.

Then she gave Dad another big sloppy kiss.

She kept the horse beside her at the table and tried to find him a name. Call him Lal, the woman said. Call him Lal, after me.

But she didn't want to do that, call him after someone with a yakky face, but she didn't want to be rude either. So she said, I can't call him Lal. Lal is a girl's name and he's a boy horse.

She wouldn't let go of the horse. They went to two more pubs, then back to Myo's and she wouldn't even go to the toilet. They drove home down the bendy road where Dad always showed her how if you look down you can see all the lights of Dublin, and if you look up you can see all the sky of the world.

She sat on the front seat with her horse in her hand and every time she slipped off the seat, the horse slipped too, and once she flew right off and banged her head on the cubby-hole where Dad keeps his Silvermints. And the horse banged his head too, so Dad stopped the car and rubbed her on the forehead; then he rubbed the horse on the head as well until they were both better.

Dad asked her if she wanted a Silvermint to help her stop crying. But she said no because, even though they look nice, they always start stinging you the minute they get into your mouth.

Why do you eat stingy Silvermints Dad?

Because they take the smell of porter away.

Why do you want to take the smell of porter away?

Because the bold policeman doesn't like it.

Dad pointed up at the roundy-o moon. Look, he said, can you see?

See what Dad – the roundy-o moon?

No. Not the moon. The man. The man on the moon. There he is, look, up there walking around.

What's his name Dad?

Nobody knows. He mightn't even have one at all.

But he doesn't care. There he is having a nice little ramble for himself around the moon.

I can't see him! I can't! I can't see him!

That's because you're not looking properly. Calm down and follow my finger – see … ?

She followed Dad's finger with her eye. She followed it slowly from the big knuckle up and when she got to the top of his finger, she saw it was tipping the moon.

Mam said, Did you have a nice time and what did you do?

She said, I drank a little pint and I went to the hotel and a woman called Lal gave Dad a big sloppy kiss and wanted him to take off his shirt upstairs and look what the barman in Myo's gave me for going to the bookies all on my own across the big road look at my horse and he banged his head when we flew off the seat in the front of the car but he's better now because Dad gave the two of our heads a rub and we saw this man walking around the moon and and and –

And Mam said, WHAT?

Then Dad said she was a big fat tell-taler.

And she said, I am NOT.

Dad said, Yes you are so, you're always telling, you even told when you were lost at the races.

No I did not, I said I *wasn't* lost.

Big tell-tale-tattler. Tell-tale-tattler. You're not my pal anymore. You'll have to stay home with Mam in future.

Then she started crying and saying, I am your pal! I am your pal! with the tears popping out of her eyes. And Dad said he was only joking. But it was too late because he'd already said it. He already said that she wasn't his pal.

Tell-tale-tattler. Tell-tale-tatty. And then it turned into Tatty on its own.

1966

DAD ONLY GIVES OUT TO YOU IF YOU'RE REALLY BOLD, but when Dad gives out, you still feel like crying even though he doesn't give you a smack. He only pretends to.

He puts his hand over your hand and smacks himself instead and you know by his face he's only messing. But you still feel like crying anyway. When Mam smacks you, you only cry if she gives you a really good wallop for yourself, and if Mam gives out to you, you only cry if she says she's going to tell Dad.

Most of the time she forgets because by the time Dad comes home she might be too busy watching telly or else be fast asleep in bed.

If Brian is extra bold she might tell on him. She might say, Wait till you hear what that fella's after doing on me now, and then she tells. But sometimes Dad says he doesn't believe her. He says he knows Brian wouldn't do such a bold thing because he's such a good boy. And that isn't fair because it's like as if he's saying Mam's telling lies.

If Brian does something really bold, he says it was Minty. Minty is his friend who lives in the garage. Brian blames Minty on all the bold things: the broken hairdryer and the cut-up knickers. The scribbles on Tatty's sums book. The blobs of white paint all over the sideboard. The wee in the coal scuttle. The wee in Mam's good high-heels.

When Brian blames Minty, Dad might say, Just wait'll I get my hands on that Minty fella. I'll wring his bloody neck for him.

And that isn't fair either because nobody else has a Minty to blame.

One time Dad got cross but and you'd know he wasn't messing. That was the time he made everyone cry. That was the time Tatty sneaked off miles away to Crumlin.

ભ

She sneaked off miles away to Crumlin with the fatbaby next door squashed into his pram, and the fatbaby's big sister called Majella Curtis. Mam was showing Mrs Curtis Lukey's new tooth over the garden wall, the two of them pressing around his gums with the tips of their little fingers. Tatty kept nagging them about being bored, so in the end they said she could bring the pram as far as the corner, seeing as how they were wrapped up warm and the winter sun was shining. They said she could be in charge, because she was the eldest. Then Jeannie said she wanted to go too and, even though that made her the eldest by one year, ten months and one week, Mam *still* said Tatty could be in charge because she had the idea first. Then Jeannie was raging.

Tatty thought she was all great pretending to be Mam, fussing over the fatbaby, making him lie down one second, then sit up again the next, shoving his soother in and out of his mouth and saying to Jeannie and Majella Curtis, Come on you pair, stop dawdling – do you hear me now? I haven't got all shagginwell day.

When they got to the corner, there was another corner and another one after that. So Tatty kept pushing the pram. Down past the far shops past the old quarry and the row of lumpy cottages and Dino's chipper and the Submarine Bar and the old red-brick school and the little brown prefab one where Tatty was in High Babies and the church made out of sparkly brick where Majella Curtis was bridesmaid for her uncle's wife from England that she couldn't remember the name of anymore. And then they were in Crumlin.

Guess what? Majella goes.

What?

My Nanny lives around here.

She does not! Where around here?

You go down that road, then another road and you see me Nanny's roundabout and it's just there.

I know! Tatty said. Why don't we go on a visit?

Tatty loved Majella Curtis's granny because she was a funny little granny and you'd think she was a little girl the way she went on except for her old grannyface. But the best thing about the little granny was she always had sweets in her pocket.

It took ages to find the little granny's house because all the roads kept getting mixed up and every road had its own exact same roundabout.

They had to keep walking, walking and Tatty kept talking, talking, like she was Mam again, about what she was getting in for the dinner and how they better all behave themselves and not make a show of her when they went on the visit. And it took ages for the little granny to open the door. She kept peeping out the letter box and squealing, Who is it? Who is it? I'm not openin' up unless you tell me your name.

And she couldn't hear what they were saying when they all said their names.

But after a while she let them in anyway.

She made them tea in big stripy mugs with shovels of shiny sugar tumbling down. She gave them hairy cinnamon drops out of her pinny pocket. Then she made lemon curd sandwiches. First she buttered the bread in her hand, then she plopped the lemon curd in the middle, next she folded the bread over and pressed it in. The lemon curd squirted out the sides, and the little granny licked all her fingers.

When it was time to go the little granny stood at the door, waving goodbye. She kept on shouting, Yoohoo! Yoo-hoo!, as if they were only coming up the road instead of going back down it. It was pitch black outside and freezing cold, so it looked like they were all smoking cigarettes, even the baby in the pram. Then they started laughing because that was so funny watching the fatbaby smoking his head off. But the fatbaby didn't think it was funny and started screaming and getting on Tatty's nerves so when they got back to the Submarine Bar she went inside to the curly barman and asked him to phone Dad. But Dad wasn't home yet. So the curly barman had to put the pram on his roof rack and drive them there himself.

When they got home, the snots were frozen hanging down out of the baby's nose or sideways stuck to his cheeks; his nappy was sapping, hanging down to his knees. And Jeannie's fingers were stuck together, her hands held out like claws. She kept on screaming, They're not my hands! They're not my hands!

So Mam had to put gloves on them and put them under her jumper and rub them and rub them until they forgot about being stuck with the cold to the handlebars of the pram and remembered how to be Jeannie's hands again.

Mrs Curtis gave out stink to Tatty, and Mam said, Oh I'm terrible sorry Mrs Curtis, I'll murder her, I really will. Mrs Curtis still kept on giving out and after a while Mam said, Ah here now, she's not *that* much older, you know, she is only just gone six – you're talking as if she's a fully grown adult. I mean to say now Mrs Curtis, let's be realistic here, when you think about it, the only actual adult involved was *your* mother. But then Majella Curtis started bawling her eyes out saying, She made me go, she made me go and she was laughin' at me Nanny AND me baby brother as well callin' him fatso every minute and tryin' to pull his cheeks out of his face.

So Mam said, Oh I'm terrible sorry Mrs Curtis, again.

When Dad came home from the races Tatty was in for it. He woke her up to give out to her.

He stood at the door holding the steak for his dinner up in his hand. There were dots of blood dripping out of the steak all over Dad's shoes, all over the floor.

Do you know the police were out looking for you? Do you know that?

No Dad, can you tell me tomorrow because I'm very tired?

Are you now? Are you? Well, do you see that steak? he goes, wagging the steak all over the place. Do you see that steak?

Yes, Dad.

The next time you do something like that, I'll give you such a hiding your ARSE is going to look like that steak.

And then Tatty couldn't stop crying. She tried to say something but the sobs wouldn't let her voice come out of her throat. She tried to say, That's very rude, you're not supposed to say that rude word – you're supposed to say *bottom* instead.

And everyone started crying, because that was the crossest anyone ever saw Dad before, and because nobody ever heard him shouting like that, except maybe through the wall at Mam.

But he still didn't give her a smack.

1967

AUNT WINNIE COMES AFTER YOU WITH
the sloppy slipper up the stairs.

The slipper snaps you on the legs. And it
sounds like the slipper can talk because every
time it gives you a snap you can hear a voice
coming out behind you.

Getup … Getup … those … bloodystairs.
Or I'll … Getup … I said … NOW this minute!

Sometimes she gives you a puck on the arm.
She throws up her hands and screams, I'll wool
the head off you. Christ I'll swing for you. You
bloodylittleblaggards I'll crucify you to the cross.

But she only ever gives you a puck on the
arm, or maybe a quick flick of the dishcloth
when you run past her.

Aunt Winnie's husband has a moustache.
Dad says it's a little mouse over his lip and
that makes you afraid in case he might ask
you for a kiss goodnight and then you might
get a bite off the mouse. Aunt Winnie's husband said Tatty has funny colour hair because

when she was a baby Mam left her out all night in the rain and that's why she went rusty. He said that's what her freckles really were, little rust marks that wouldn't wash off her face.

She tried to write a letter to Mam to tell her she hated her for leaving her out in the rain and making her go rusty. But she didn't know how to write a letter yet, so she drew a picture of Mam instead. With her eyes turning in and spots all over her face and big lumps of poo running all down her legs.

Then Aunt Winnie's husband made Tatty read out of the newspaper.

Now! he goes to the big cousins. What do you think of that? Eh? Eh? What have you got to say for yourselves now? She's only in first class and able to read. And look at you lot. You big useless lumps.

Another aunty is Betty. She has a cane hanging on a nail behind the kitchen door. She takes it down and gives it a wobble. When she gives it a wobble the cane goes *whuck!*

She has an apple tree out her back garden and crusts of bread outside her back door for the birds' dinner. Aunt Betty says you're not supposed to eat anything off the ground because you'll be sick and then you might die. But the crusts don't make you sick and the crusts don't make you die. Aunt Betty's husband never gives out or says that she's rusty. He brings home chocolate on Friday and sends you up a few chips in bed and sometimes he cuts you a long slow slice of cheese from his special block that no one else is allowed to eat only him and Tatty.

Aunt Betty takes the cane down and says, Will I give those bowsies a good wallop for themselves across the back of the legs? And then Tatty doesn't know what to say. Because it might be good to hear what the cane sounds like when it wallops a leg instead of only the air. But it might hurt too much as well.

Then there's Aunt June. Aunt June thinks Tatty is a silly name. So she calls her Caroline instead.

Aunt June doesn't smack you but she sends you up to your room. Except it's not your room because it's in her house, and the big cousins are all in school, and the one with pink lipstick and the flick in her hair is in work, so that means you have the room all to yourself.

You can look at their comics and mess with their stuff. You can open the vanity case and look at the lipstick and the hairnet with the pink and blue curlers for making the flick tucked up inside. You can stand on the bed and read the funny names of all the people in the pictures on the wall. You can wonder why the boys have two names each: Gene Pitney, Herman Hermit. But the girls only have one: Lulu, Cilla. Or the one with the black face that's called Milly.

Aunt June is the strictest aunty even though she wouldn't curse at you or give you a smack. She's cross if you mumble or bang on the piano or smudge your fingers on the furniture or forget to flush the chain. If she sends you out to the shops and you get chocolate biscuits instead of Marietta, she'll make you go back. And it doesn't matter how much you beg her or if you start crying or pretend you're after getting sick, she'll still make you go back and change them.

But the one thing that Aunt June really can't stand is lies, so that's why Tatty gets into the most trouble with her.

I've a good mind to put mustard in your mouth, Aunt June says, if you tell me any more of your lies.

But that wouldn't matter to Tatty. Because one time Dad put mustard on her thumb to stop her from sucking it and making her teeth go buck. And she wouldn't come in for her tea for Mam, sitting on the doorstep watching Mr Curtis mowing his lawn. Watching the grass burst out of the twirly blades and Mr Curtis's welly boots walking slowly behind, his bumpy bare elbows swinging away from him. Then coming back into him again. With her special soft pillow plopped down on her head, fingers pressing *plick!* sounds out of the fat bit hanging down, mouth on her thumb suck-ingsucking away, eyes getting dizzy with shreds of soft green and flicks of white daisies, Mr Curtis's lawnmower growling roundandroundandround in her head.

So that's why it wouldn't matter to Tatty, because the mustard made her thumb taste like a little lump of ham. And then it made her fall fast asleep without knowing it. Sometimes it's not her fault when she tells lies. Sometimes the big cousins make her, lying in bed in the dark.

They say, Tell us something good that happened during the week.

Like what?

Anything at all, something that happened when you were out with your Dad.

Nothing happened.

Ah you're no good. Go on asleep then, you're no good at all.

And that was a bit lonely lying in the dark with no cousins to talk to and that was a bit scary as well, because the best part about staying with the cousins was all the words coming out in the dark, until you fell fast asleep without knowing. Instead of lying awake on your own at home, listening to Deirdre grinding her teeth or Brian chewing his thumb or wheezy Jeannie whispering her prayers then falling asleep the minute she said amen. Or listening for things outside the room, like the sounds of the telly or the sound of Dad's car coming in the gate or the sound of Mam and Dad talking to each other, or sometimes the sound of them not speaking.

Listening and listening.

I'm trying, I am, she said to the cousins. I'm trying to remember something good that happened, I swear I am.

But nobody answered. Letting on snores, letting on to be asleep.

Then she remembered! A funny house made out of wood that she saw when she was in a place called Leixlip with Dad, with wooden steps and a sort of a stage going round the front of the house that Dad said was called a veranda.

I saw this house.

What kind a house?

It was a … a cowboy house.

And … ?

And it was no good telling them about the house on its own, she had to make the house have a story. So she looked into the dark until she saw the house and she stared at the house until the door swung open and a man dressed in black stepped out on the veranda.

I met the Virginian!

The Virginian? Off the telly? Go away! What was he like?

If I tell you, you won't tell anyone else?

No. No. Swear we won't. Holy bible. Swear it.

Tell your Aunty Juney the story about the Virginian.

What story?

You know, the one you told us last night in bed.

I didn't –

Yes you did.

Well I can't remember.

Yes you can – about Trampus and Betsy and what Trampus said to your dad – ah go on, you can.

No, I can't.

Well, *I'll* tell it then, one of the big cousins said in the end.

But the big cousin made such a mess of the story, skipping the best bits, saying it too quick, mixing it all up, bursting out laughing when it wasn't even funny. So Tatty had to take the story back and tell it herself. Her face was all red when she was telling the story because everyone was laughing and every time she looked over at Aunt June, Aunt June's eyes were looking back and she knew they didn't believe her.

When she was finished Aunt June went *tut* and gave out to the cousins. You're worse, she said, encouraging her like that.

Ah for God's sake Mammy, the cousin with the flick said, it's only a bit of fun.

Fun or not, Aunt June said, one of these days those lies of hers are going to get her into right trouble.

Ah she won't tell any more lies – sure you won't Tatty? the cousin with the flick said.

Oh no. I'm never going to. Never again. Ever.

But the next day she told two whoppers.

The first was after she was caught out crossing the big road on her own.

You could have been knocked down, *killed* even. Then what would I say to your father?

He lets me cross the big road on my own. He does. The one beside Myo's.

That's *another* bare-faced lie! Aunt June said.

Anyway I didn't cross it, Tatty said, I went over the bridge.

What bridge? There's no bridge.

There is so.

The more Aunt June said there was no bridge, the more Tatty could see it. It had trees and flowers and a special place for people to walk with black and white stripes and a green bench where if you got too tired you could stop and have a little rest. And she could see her sandals going over the stripes and when she looked over the side of the bridge she could see right down on Dorset Street; the long tops of all the buses and the square tops of all the cars, ducking under the bridge.

Right! Aunt June goes. We'll sort this out for once and for all. Then she dragged Tatty by the sleeve of her anorak down the road so she could show her where the bridge was.

Tatty couldn't believe it when she got to the place and the bridge was gone.

Now? Aunt June said. Now? What have you got to say for yourself?

It must have –

It must have what?

It must have fallen down in the storm.

What storm? There WASN'T any storm.

I'm sorry Aunt June.

Now I'm warning you Miss. That was your last chance – do you hear me? Your. *Very*. Last. Chance.

The second lie she told was when Dad's new manager came to collect her.

But I was expecting himself, Aunt June says. I mean, nobody said anything to me. I mean, I've never seen you before. I mean –

That's quite all right Madam, the little one knows me well – isn't that so my dear?

Do you Caroline? Do you know this man?

Tatty looked at Dad's new manager's big smiley teeth. Then she looked at Aunt June's eyes, and she knew they didn't believe him.

Do you know him, I'm asking you? Aunt June said. Will you answer me please?

I don't know. I mean I don't think so. I mean, no. And first Dad's new manager was very nice, laughing away with his big smiley teeth, calling Aunt June Madam, tossing Tatty's hair and saying, Oh you little scamp. But then he got fed up with her telling her lies and started shouting at her and calling her a bold brat. Then it was Aunt June's turn to go mad. She said she couldn't allow her niece to go with the man if she didn't

even know who he was and who did he think he was
shouting at a little child like that, and besides which he
had some nerve presenting himself at her door with a
smell of drink off him, he could be anybody. *Anybody.*
He could be that Ian Brady for all she knew. Then she
closed the door in his face.

Aunt June?

Mmm?

Aunt June?

What?

Who's Ian Brady?

Never you mind. But you never, ever go with strangers.
Even if it's a woman stranger, do you hear me? Never, ever.
Even if they offer you sweets. Even if they say they know
you or your mammy or daddy. Never, *ever.*

Yes, Aunt June.

You're sure now, you didn't know him?

When Aunt June found out Tatty had told more of her lies,
she was raging so much she was nearly crying. She said that
was the end of the last chances; she never wanted Tatty to
stay in her house again because if there was one thing she
couldn't tolerate – it was what?

Lies, Aunt June.

Lies *and* liars. What's wrong with you anyway? What in
the name of God is wrong with you?

I just …

You just what?

I just didn't want to go home.

Didn't want to go to school more like.

No. I swear.

To tell such lies right up to that man's face, right up to his *face*. The audacity of it, the sheer … You're seven years old for God's sake. You've even made your first holy communion. I can't get over it. I just … *Why?* Why do you do it? Why do you keep telling lies?

I don't know, Tatty said. They just come into my head.

Well, STOP them coming into your head then. Think before you speak.

I can't stop them, she said. They just come in by themselves.

అ

Mam has other sisters as well, but Winnie, Betty and June are the ones you know best because they're the ones who mind you. She has a few brothers too. She even has a secret brother who lives in a hospital. But you're not allowed talk about him until you're old enough to understand and then Mam says she'll tell you all about him. But in the meantime, she says, you're not to so much as mention him in front of the cousins, especially that granny one Pauline.

But why Mam?

Because some of them were told he died in the war.

What war? I didn't see any war.

Ah years ago, before you were born. Just don't mention him, that's all.

But why do they think he died in the war?

Because that's what their mams want them to think

But why?

Because *that's* the why.

Can I just ask his name Mam?

No.

Please Mam? I just want to know his name.

All right then, Richie.

Richie? My Uncle Richie?

Yes, Richie, your uncle Richie. My brother Richard.

Dad has other brothers and sisters as well but he doesn't speak to them, so you might be able to find out what your other cousins are called, but you wouldn't know what they look like or what it's like to play with them.

The only one he speaks to is Aunt Sal. She's his little sister. Her house has the nicest smell.

Aunt Sal doesn't think Dad's house has a nice smell but. She's always giving out about it with her nose all crinkled up.

Oh for Christ's sake would you not go and buy a decent house for your family – the state of this place?

Or – I believe you've only gone and bought a racehorse? Well you'd make the cat laugh, you would, throwing your money away on gambling and drink. I know what I'd do if I was your wife.

Aunt Sal always gives cheek to Dad. And he always lets her away with it.

It's great being on your own with Aunt Sal. She lets you try on her shoes and light her cigarettes for her. She lets you have a squirt of her perfume. She says as soon as she gets a new baby she'll let you have a mind of it.

Mam says Aunt Sal's house is gorgeous because she has no kids to destroy it. She says Aunt Sal is gorgeous herself because she has feck all to do all day but doll herself up to the nines. But Aunt Sal is gorgeous because she used to be an air hostess.

She has long nails like the woman in the Oxo ad and a white sofa and a white rug that looks like a polar bear that's after getting knocked down. She has a bunful of blonde hair and a long silver comb with a sharp point on the end for poking the bun into place. She has a mini-car that she drives to the shops and a mini-skirt that's made out of suede and a fur coat that goes all the way down to her ankles. She has a husband that calls her honeybunch and kisses her on the lips right in front of you. There's a cream telephone in her hall and a plastic wardrobe in the spare room that you open with a zip instead of a door and then you can see Aunt Sal's wedding dress and her old air-hostess uniform and her old school uniform and her old girlguide uniform as well.

In her dining-room there's this long low cabinet made out of smoky glass. It has slanty legs and a record-player inside, and on one end of it there's a place for the records, on the other a press for bottles of drink. The bottles of drink all have lovely names. Aunt Sal reads them out, Cinzan-o Bianc-o. Advo-cah. Dew-bon-eh. Pimm's Number One.

Mam is the youngest in her family, the last one to get married, so all the aunties' houses have big cousins in them except for Aunt Sal's where there's no cousins at all.

But none of the houses has a special cousin, a special child. Only our house has.

Only our house has a special child called Deirdre.

1968

DEIRDRE IS A SPECIAL CHILD HOLY GOD SENT TO US because he loves us so much and knows he can trust us to look after her. He picked us out of hundreds of families, and it took him ages to make up his mind because God is very fussy about who gets his special children.

Deirdre is the eldest. She's one year older than Jeannie, three years older than Tatty, four and a half years older than Brian and a whole seven years older than Lukey. But even though she's the eldest, she can never be in charge, because she doesn't understand.

Deirdre used to screech for all sorts of reasons. Like when she was too hungry to feed herself, then Mam had to feed her instead, with two spoons so there was always one in her mouth and always one on the way. She screeched when she was too tired or when she wanted something she couldn't have, banging her toys on the floor, kicking her legs in the air.

And when she was afraid of things. Black flappy things: Batman on the telly; crows in the back garden; town when it was all rainy and she saw the black umbrellas pass over her head. Or the big tall nun at the bus-stop who bent over her go-car and said, God bless the beautiful child!

Now when she screeches, it's because she just feels like having a screechy day.

When Deirdre dribbles she gets a sore rash that creeps down her chin and all over her neck. Then you have to cover the rash up with Lassar's cream and for a while she looks like Dad when he's having a shave. But then the dribbles run down her chin and wash the Lassar's away and you can see the sore rash again.

Her dribbles come out on long silver strings and then they destroy her clothes. The tops of her jumpers are always scratchy, the collar of her coat is hard and dark, the buttonholes are stiff, so you have to push and push to make the buttons do what they're told.

Mam doesn't like Deirdre to wear bibs anymore because she's too big now and people might laugh at her. So that means Mam has to try catch the dribbles before they fall out of her mouth. When Mam opens her handbag hundreds of hankies come tumbling out, and when she takes off her coat they pop out of her sleeves. Mam is quick with the hankies but sometimes she's not quick enough. If she can't find a hankie on time she stretches over and breaks the dribbly string with her fingers.

Sometimes Deirdre has fits that make her fly across the room. Once she nearly knocked Tatty into the fire because there was no guard in front of it and Tatty jumped in the way to stop her from falling in. Tatty's skirt got singed and her face turned white, her mouth went all wobbly: *vovovo vovovovo*. She looked like she was only after getting out of the bath.

But it was Tatty's own fault, because she was the one who took the fireguard away. And she was the one who threw sugar on the fire to make it go *whooooosh* up the chimney.

When Deirdre has one of her fits, her body goes mad bouncy and her eyes turn back to front. Then you have to shout for Mam, and Mam says, Oh Jesus! Oh Christ! and comes running into the room with a spoon. She puts the spoon into Deirdre's mouth so she won't bite her tongue off. She puts her other hand under Deirdre's head to stop her from cracking it off the floor. She waits for Deirdre's arms and legs to stop bashing around.

Deirdre gets jacked out after her fit. Mam wraps her up in her blanket and holds her on her lap. She whispers, Shush-shush-shush my little lamb. Shushashush-sh.

Then Deirdre goes for her little sleep.

She's too tall for her age, but she didn't know how to walk until Dad showed her. She wore nappies until she was nearly five and Mam had to make the nappies herself out of towelling stuff you buy in Arnotts because her bum was too big for the nappies you buy for little babies. Everyone says it's an awful pity about Deirdre because she has such a beautiful face. Then they say Mam is a saint. Nobody ever says Dad is a saint. Even though he was the one who got her out of nappies and he was the one who showed her how to walk and then showed her how to turn all the funny noises she makes into words.

He stands at the far wall and says, Are you ready?

He goes down on his hunkers and says, Are you steady?

He puts his arms out to her and goes, Are you ready, are you steady? Look into my eyes, only into my eyes ... one, two, three and CHAAAARGE! Deirdre, CHAAARGE!

And she looks like she's swimming in the cold, cold sea, with her arms flapping all over the place, feet going too fast for her body, blinky eyes popping out of her head, breath all sharp and afraid.

The first time she ever walks without falling, Mam starts crying. Dad pats Deirdre on the head and says, there's my good girl, my good brave girl. And his eyes are all sad and damp when they should be happy and dry. My good girl, my good brave girl.

Then he makes her do it again.

When Deirdre hears Dad's car coming she crawls into her top secret place behind the sofa. But he always finds her and makes her practise. And practise and practise. Until one day she gets it right.

The first word she ever said was the bold F-off. Dad didn't teach her the bold F-off on purpose, she just picked it up by herself. She couldn't really say it properly but you could still tell what she meant by the way she put all the sounds together, and by the cross little face on her when she pushed the sounds out of her mouth: FUH AW.

If you said a bold word, Dad would give out to you. He'd say, Where did you hear that dirty filthy word? And then you'd have to say, I don't know Dad, even though you know you heard it off him in the car. But when Deirdre said the big F-off Dad didn't give out to her. Dad gave her a hug and a big swing up to the ceiling.

CR

This woman in a nurse's uniform calls in for a little chat.

I just called in for a little chat, she says to Mam, a chat about poor little Deirdre.

She drinks three cups of tea but only takes one tiny bite out of her Lemon Puff biscuit. Then she starts going on about a special school for Deirdre.

Excuse me for a minute, Mam goes, but are you talking about an institution?

NO! No of course not.

You are. What you're asking me to do is to put *my* child into an institution?

Oh no really, it's not like that at all, it's a proper school that caters for children with special needs, more like a home from home than anything else. Lovely rooms and –

Over my dead – Mam says.

Listen the fact of the matter is, the woman goes – making her voice low like she's going to tell Mam this big secret – you've got to think of your other children, think of the strain on them. I mean is it fair? Because you know, the older she gets the more difficult –

Over my dead – Mam says again.

Then the woman opens her bag and takes out a booklet. Well, have a read of this booklet anyway, she says. You can discuss it with your husband and let me know what he –

I don't have to discuss it with my husband, I already know how he feels.

But how – ?

Oh don't imagine for one minute that you're the first one to suggest putting her away!

She leaves the booklet and the biscuit behind her. Mam throws them both in the bin.

Mam's found something else to read instead of the nurse's booklet. Something in one of her shiny magazines. She tears the page out and puts it in the kitchen drawer. She keeps taking it out and looking at it. Then she knows it off by heart. It's all about how if you put special children into a normal school with normal children they can start to copy off them and stop being so special. There's a picture on the top of the page of another mam with another special child sitting on her lap. Mam says it makes sense when you come to think about it. I mean to say, she goes, did we ever think we'd see the day she could walk *and* nearly dress herself as well?

She says this to anyone who comes into the kitchen. She makes them all a cup of tea and shows them the page with the picture on it. She asks them what they think and her eyes get all happy when they say, Yes, it's a good idea.

Until she asks Mrs Rogers from across the road.

Mrs Rogers goes, Ah no. Ah no, you'd be wasting your time there.

I'm sorry Mrs Rogers, Mam says, I'm not sure what you mean?

Well, for a start, it's not going to cure her, is it? And what school's going to take her? Let's face it, the parents'd be bound to object. And anyway take a look at the child in the picture. He's not the same as Deirdre – is he now? He's a mongo. And they do pick up things terrible quick, you know. Oh they do be as cute, like little monkeys. Just because he's able to tie his laces and butter his bread, doesn't mean to say your Deirdre'll be.

Then Mam says she never heard such ignorance in all her life and Mrs Rogers goes, Well excuse me, I was asked for me opinion, and Mam says, Would you mind going now? And Mrs Rogers says, Would I mind? I'd be only delighted.

When Mam tells Dad about the boy in the magazine he eats his dinner and stares at the floor. His mouth goes round with the meat, his nose twitches up and down, he puts his knife and fork down on the plate, he pushes the plate away.

She tells him all about Mrs Rogers. She takes off the lazy loud way Mrs Rogers speaks through her nose and everyone laughs. Except Dad. She asks him does he not think Mrs Rogers is a common tinker? Then asks him if he ever heard such ignorance in all his life? She asks him does he not think the magazine article makes sense when you come to think about it? She asks him that again.

She stands at the sink and waits for Dad's answers.

Dad rubs his nose with the back of his hand and pours himself a glass of milk.

ᘓ

Tatty, on her way home from school, just about to get off the bus, sees Mam and Deirdre, just about to get on. They're in their best coats. Their *very* best coats.

She humps her school-bag up on her back, puts her hand on the pole and starts to step off the platform. She has a big red face because she's pretending she doesn't see them even though they're standing right beside her. *Right beside her.* Best coats on. That's them just there.

Mam says, Excuse me Miss, and where do you think you're going?

She says, Oh hello, Mam. I'm just on my way home.

But Mam says she is in her barney. Mam says she has to get back on the bus.

But why?

We're going to see the teacher.

But Mam I'm only after –

I need you to mind Deirdre while I talk to the teacher.

But the teacher's not there, school's over.

No it's not. The big class doesn't finish till three. Anyway it's the Head Teacher I want to see.

But *Mam*.

Mam won't tell Tatty why they have to go back on the bus, but with her wanting to see the Head Teacher and the good coats and all, she's able to guess that it probably has something to do with Mam's big plan. Her plan to send Deirdre to Tatty's school.

Mam looks out the window; her lips are barely moving but they don't make any sound. It's like she's talking to someone inside her head. Tatty tries to get Mam to talk to her instead. She tells Mam all about what she'll see when she gets to the school.

There'll be this big yard, she says, and on one side of the yard there'll be a long brown building made out of wood that says *Buachaillí* over the door and on the other side there'll be the same kind of building that says *Cailíní*. *Buachaillí* means boys and *cailíní* means girls. Did you know that Mam – did you?

And the gate will be closed so you'll have to ring the bell and then maybe someone from sixth class will come out and open it. Or maybe the Head Teacher herself. If it is the Head Teacher she'll be wearing a pink cardigan and a grey dress. There'll be a silver whistle hanging around her neck. That's how you'll know her. Are you listening Mam – are you?

Mam stops looking out the window when they get near the stop for the school. But she still doesn't speak. She's too busy fixing Deirdre's clothes and going mad with the hankies every minute. For the whole journey the only words to come out of her mouth are the one-and-two-halves-to-Crumlin-please that she says to the busman. Or when she stuffs a few hankies into Tatty's pockets and tells her she has to keep Deirdre tidy while she talks to the teacher.

When Mam says you have to keep Deirdre tidy, that means you're in charge of the dribbles.

Mam talks to the Head Teacher out in the yard. Tatty holds Deirdre's hand and stands at the prefab wall. Out through the wall you can hear the big class screaming; you can hear the chairs scraping off the floor, can feel the wooden wall rumble at your back. Sometimes the Head Teacher leaves Mam to come over to the wall and give it a good thump for itself. *Ciúnas*, she says and there's quiet for a minute, but as soon as she walks back to Mam the walls start rumbling again.

Tatty can't hear what the Head Teacher is saying, but she knows by her face she doesn't want Deirdre in her brown school. And she knows by the way she keeps putting her hand up to interrupt Mam that she doesn't want to hear about Mam's big plan.

Mam tries to tell her about all the things she read in the magazine. She even tries to make the Head Teacher take the page so she can read it herself. She points at the picture of the other mam with the other special child sitting on her lap. But the Head Teacher doesn't want the page. Her hand goes up again, and this time it stays up until Mam folds the page up again and puts it back in her handbag.

Then half of Tatty hates the Head Teacher for not wanting Deirdre. But the other half is glad as well. Because she knows Deirdre wouldn't be able to sit still on the little chair all day or wipe her blackboard or polish her desk. And anyway her desk would be all messy with dribbles and then she might have one of her fits. And Tatty would have to mind her all day so that means she wouldn't be able to be on her own.

And she likes going to school on her own on the bus, holding her penny bus fare for the way home in her hand all day, checking every now and then, the rust mark it leaves on her palm. And she likes opening her little bottle of milk, eating her sandwiches sitting in her coat on the bench in the yard, watching the different gangs charge up and down. And she's glad Mam didn't take her out when the new big school up the road was finished, even though Jeannie's been going there since last September and everybody keeps on saying it would be easier if the two of them were in the same school. Mam still said Tatty could stay where she was because it would be a shame to move her from her little brown school that she loved so much.

When the teacher says, *Té a codhladh*, that means it's time to go for a sleep on your desk with your arms folded into a pillow. Everything so quiet you can hear outside: the buses passing, the boys' toilet flushing, the teacher blowing smoke from her sneaky cigarette.

But there wouldn't be any *té a codhladh* if Deirdre was there because Deirdre might start screeching and the Head Teacher might hear her and come in. Then Deirdre might say the big F-off and, even though she can't say it properly, the Head Teacher might still know what she means.

Because the Head Teacher knows everything about everything, and all sorts of things. The rivers and mountains all over the world; the names of all the men on the teacloth who died for Ireland; the words of all the poems in the book. And the Head Teacher knows how to play the harmonica and how to turn a heel in a sock. The Head Teacher knows everything and everything. The Head Teacher just knows.

She wants to shout out to Mam: Come on Mam, don't ask her anymore. Come on let's go home.

She wants to shout out to Mam: Come on Mam, leave my little brown school alone. There's more room in Jeannie's big green school – why can't you ask there instead?

And that's the way Tatty always is with Deirdre: halvohalvo.

One minute she's punching the big boy round the corner for jeering her big sister. Punching and kicking at him, going, *You're* the spa. You're the big spa. Dumdum *yourself.* Dumdum your own fat self.

And he's twice the size of her, dragging her all the way down the road by the hair. But she doesn't care, she still wouldn't let anyone jeer her sister.

Then the next minute she's hiding up the lane so she won't have to bring Deirdre to the shop. Or else she's pretending Deirdre's Spanish on the bus and that's why she talks so funny.

She wants to squeeze the guts out of her because she loves her so much.

She hates her because she won't learn anything you try to show her.

Like how to hang up a coat, tie her own shoelaces, brush her own hair. No matter how slow you go, she just won't learn. Then Tatty ends up screaming crying, banging her fists off the bed, Why can't you just listen? Why can't you ever just listen? You're holding the hairbrush the wrong way round. *The wrong way round.* And you brush your hair *down*, not UP. *Down* not UP.

But then she loves her again and just wants to hug her all day, putting plaits in her hair in the garden.

On the way home from the school they go upstairs on the bus, so no one will see Mam crying.

The busman whistles up the stairs. The busman stops when he sees Mam crying. He goes back down the stairs again and lets them off with the bus fare.

Then Tatty hates Mam for making a show of them. And Mam's stupid handbag with the stupid magazine picture folded up inside. And Mam's stupid scarf, and her stupid face underneath it, all squashed up and dripping with tears.

When they get off the bus she takes Deirdre by the hand and they both walk on ahead so no one will know they're with stupid Mam.

෬

In the end Mam does find a special school for Deirdre. With a special bus to bring her there every morning and bring her home again at about three.

The first time Deirdre saw the bus she started scream-ing. She threw herself on the ground kicking her legs all over the place. She got a hold of Mam's legs and wouldn't let go. And then the man who drove the bus had to get down, pull her away from Mam's legs and lift her onto the bus. She stopped screaming then, just frightened little mouse-squeaks instead.

Mam please, Brian said, she doesn't want to go. Please Mam.

But she has to go love.

But she doesn't want to, she doesn't like it.

She'll get to like it.

Do you promise Mam?

Yes, I promise, Mam said.

And Brian must have believed Mam when she said that because then he stopped crying.

Tatty looked at all the other children through the spe-cial-bus window.

And some of them looked like eskimos out of the *Children from Around the World* book and some of them looked like old people who were so tired they just wanted to sleep and sleep and a few of them were rocking them-selves side to side or backwards and forwards.

One girl kept bashing her head off the seat in front. There was a piece of foam tied around her forehead. The foam had a stain of blood. And there was this other boy who couldn't stop laughing at nothing even though it was nearly making him get sick.

Tatty walked over to the bus and touched Deirdre's face through the window.

I'm sorry Deedee, she said. I'm sorry I am.

1969

MAM SAYS EVERYONE FALLS OUT, NOT JUST HER and Dad.

She says it's a sign you love someone, because you wouldn't be bothered having a row with somebody you just didn't care about – now would you?

No Mam.

It's nothing to be ashamed of you know.

Yes Mam.

But that doesn't mean you have to go broadcasting it either.

Mam doesn't call them fights, she calls them little rows.

You had a little row with Jeannie yesterday – doesn't mean you don't love her, does it? And in school you have little rows with your friends?

Me? I do NOT.

Why are you laughing? Why is that so funny?

It just is. I don't have rows in school. But here – there's these two best friends in my class and they're always, always –

There now! And I bet they make friends again, don't they? Of course they do. Well, so do me and Dad. We get very cross with each other, then we have our little row, but in the end we make it up again because we love each other. It's the same thing really, only the people are bigger. The exact same thing – do you see?

Yes Mam.

But she doesn't see, not really. She sees little bits that might be the same, but too many big bits that are different.

Say if two best friends in your class fall out they might just get in a huff and stop speaking. But say if they lose their tempers and go a bit mental they won't care who sees or hears them. They hit each other out in the yard, they pull each other's hair in the classroom. Then they say loads of mean things to each other. The mean things they say don't even have to be true; it can be something about your house or your family, if you have no car or maybe no phone. It can be about your skinniness or your fatness. Or it can just be something like – I hate you, I hope you get flattened by a bigbus. I never want to be your friend again, you stupid smelly greasy-hair bitch.

After a while the two best friends make it up again, nobody remembers how. Even they mightn't remember if you ask them. It just happens by itself.

If you have a fight with someone in the house, one of your cousins, or a brother or sister, Dad makes you say sorry and shake hands. He makes you shake hands even though you're still not speaking yet. You can't look at the face you're supposed to say sorry to so you look down at the hand you're shaking instead. You want to squeeze the guts out of the hand till it breaks. You want to give it a bite and then get sick on top of it. Dad doesn't care. He still makes you shake hands. He still makes you say you're sorry.

But when Mam and Dad have a fight nobody makes *them* shake hands. They're allowed to fight for as long as they want. They're allowed to go on and on, until they're ready to stop by themselves. On and on, they can even spend a whole summer having the same fight, if that's what they feel like.

℣

It rips through the house in the middle of the night, huge like a train.

It wakes you up with its screeches and screams, curses and roars.

It bashes itself off the living-room wall. It flings things SMASH off the fireplace. It whacks and wallops and cracks and slams until bit by bit it tires itself out, and that means the first big fight is over.

Then they're not speaking.

Maybe weeks and maybe months; they won't speak again until after they've had the second big fight. Because the second big fight means they're ready to give in.

Unless something really big happens first, like if somebody dies, your Granny maybe or Dad's best friend. Or somebody has to go into hospital: Jeannie if her asthma gets too bad; Brian if he falls off the roof; Mam if she takes too many tablets by mistake.

But mostly it's after the second big fight. You just have to wait that's all.

You keep on thinking there's a funny smell in the house. When you come home from school you sniff your nose around but the house just smells like it always does. And that just drives you mad because even though your nose can't find it, you know it's there, you feel it's there – it's like a smell without a smell.

ᚙ

Dad draws you a picture. It only takes him a few seconds with the pencil flying all over the page. He draws you a picture of a horse. There, he says, it's hardly Arkle but it'll have to do.

She shows Dad's horse to Mam. She wants the horse to make Mam like Dad again. Mam says yes, it's a beautiful horse and yes, Dad is a very good drawer.

Then Tatty gets this great idea. She asks Mam to draw a horse too, so she can show Dad and maybe when he sees Mam's horse that might make him like Mam again. But Mam's horse looks stupid. It's more like a dog or a cat and everything about it is square and flat, even the tail.

Ah Ma-am.

What?

Ah that's no good. Can you not make it look like a real horse – look, like the one Dad made?

Then Mam turns mental in a minute and throws the pencil on the floor.

You and your oulfella, you and your bloody oulfella, I'm sick to the teeth of the pair of you. Get out of my sight.

But Mam. I was only –

Ah you're always only. Always only. Think you're so bloody clever. Talking to me as if I'm a thick. Jeannie has *twice* your brains and she'd never dream of speaking to me like that. Just like your oulfella. Looking down your nose at me. And you can stop that whingeing or I'll give you something to whinge about.

But Mam … ?

Stop it, I said. Unless you're looking for a smack? Are you? Are you looking for a smack? Is that what you want? Is it? Is it?

No thank you Mam.

No thank you Mam. Get out of my sight, you make me sick. Go on. GO!

ଔ

She sits up in the top bunk bawling her brains out. BANG goes her head off the wooden partition, SCREECH flies her voice up to the ceiling. Bang. Scream. Screech. Bang. Louder and louder. Louder than them in the end, that's why they can hear her.

Stop fighting stop fighting you're giving me a headache. You're giving me a headache stop fighting stop fighting. Stop headache headache stopitstopit. STAAW-AWP.

Mam stays at the door with her face inside the shadow. Dad comes in and stands beside the bed. He rubs her head to calm her down. He says she can suck her thumb if she wants. Then he says, Shh, listen – can you hear?

Hear what?

It's stopped.

Does that mean it's gone away Dad?

Yes, I sent it away. And here's a big fat promise for you – I'm never going to let it come back in this house again.

It wasn't a little row Dad.

No sweetheart it wasn't.

Mam might say it was a little row, but it wasn't.

Maybe it started as a little row.

Then what happened?

It just got too big for its boots, I suppose.

Mam and Dad go back out to the living-room and everything is quite again. All you can hear is the ticktock clock. Tick and then tock. And the sound Tatty always makes when she cries too much, Hee-haw. Hee and then haw. Slower and slower until she falls back asleep. Like as if she has the hiccups. Or as if she's a donkey instead of a little girl.

CR

When Mam and Dad make friends again, Dad buys Mam a big bunch of flowers and drives her into town and gives her money for lovely new clothes. And Mam calls that going on a spree. Then he buys her dinner in a posh restaurant and brings her away for the weekend and brings her to the races and into the pubs in town so she has somewhere nice to show off her new clothes and everyone's happy, laughing and laughing all over the place.

Then Dad breaks his fat promise and lets the fight come back in the house.

Then they're not speaking *again*.

You don't see that much of Dad. When you do see him, he's different, like he's your uncle instead of your Dad. He puts down his paper when you come into the room, asks you about school and how are you keeping. He sends you to the shops to buy the papers and instead of just giving you a tip for yourself, he lets you keep all the change.

He draws you a picture and helps you with your homework. On Sunday he tells everyone to be in the car in five minutes. Then he says it's Brian's turn to sit in the front seat. When he says that you know Mam isn't coming.

Where are we going Dad?

We're going for a drive in the country then I'm going to bring you somewhere nice for dinner.

(What about Mam?)

Jeannie is the biggest brainy-box in her class. She's good at everything she does: sums, English, Irish, spellings; she even gets an A in knitting and sewing. On the wallchart in her classroom, there's so many gold stars squashed beside her name it looks like a gold-star gorilla. She's clever at things outside school too, like she's able to make a proper dinner with potatoes and meat and gravy. She fixes the telly and tidies the presses so you can see where everything is instead of just making your arm guess, poking it in. She polishes all the shoes and makes all the lunches; does all the housework for making Mam in a good humour again. She hates anything that's not perfect. That's why she hates her own hands because they keep growing warts on the sly. She wastes her pocket money on buying plasters for covering the warts during the day. At night she paints the warts with smelly stuff that looks like nail varnish.

But the cleverest thing about Jeannie is she knows how to speak without making a sound.

She can mime words with her mouth and hands; she can make her eyebrows and eyes boss you around. She can pull her little notebook out of her pocket and write you the teeniest message that she scribbles out real quick before anyone else sees it.

She fits her mouth into your ear and pushes her voice right inside your head. When she fits her mouth into your ear it makes a long tickle go down your neck and all down your side. Then her voice wiggles around the inside of your head and nobody else in the world can hear it. *What about Mam's dinner?* it asks Tatty. *What about Mam?*

I don't know.

You don't know what, Tatty? asks Dad from the front of the car.

Nothin' Dad.

You must know somethin'. Everyone knows somethin'.

Jeannie's eyes start twirling around; her eyebrows jump up and down. *Ask him*, they say. *Go on. Ask.*

Hey Dad?

Yeah?

Can I ask you something?

Of course you can. Ask me anything you like.

Well, what about – ? I mean, what was I going to say again? I mean, how is – ? Em, whatdoyoucallit? Mam! What about Mam's dinner? What about Mam?

What about her? he says.

Mam is different too. You see her all the time, all the days, and she's either really sad or else in really bad humour.

Sometimes when she's sad she might ask Brian for a hug. The hug is too tight and nearly squashes his guts out. Ow, he says, ow, you're hurting me Mam. She doesn't say sorry for hurting him, she just pushes him out of the way. And then she's in bad humour again.

She cries when she's talking to the aunties on the phone; she cries in the kitchen on her own. And that makes you feel really sorry for poor old Mam, crying on her own in the kitchen when she's trying to make the dinner or wash the dishes or sort out all the clothes.

But then after a while she stops being sad and doesn't cry anymore: she just stays in bad humour all the time. Then you don't feel sorry for Mam. You just feel afraid.

ରେ

There's a right pong in the bedroom: poo all over the cot; mashed into his hair; streaked over his legs, arms; there's even flicks of it under his fingernails. Lukey's taken his nappy off again; Mam is giving him such a hiding.

It's in the middle of one of Deirdre's screechy days. It's in the middle of a big long fight she's having with Dad. You can hear the slaps all over the house. You can hear the long screams of Lukey. Even from behind the sofa you can hear them.

Slap! Slap! Take that. That. And here's another one for you. And another. *Slap! Slap!* You. Dirty. Filthy. Little. *Slap!*

That's why Tatty runs into the bedroom, even though Jeannie begs her not to, trying to pull her back by the elbow, whispering into her ear, *Don't Tatty don't Tatty don't.*

But Tatty does. She runs into the bedroom shouting her head off at Mam,

You leave him alone. You leave him alone or I'm straight telling my Daddy on *you*.

Then Mam really goes mad. She'll bloodywell smack who she likes, whenever. And she'll smack Tatty too, give her such a crack across the face, mark her for life, if she doesn't shut up and mind her own business. She's warning her now. She's warning her.

You leave him alone, you leave my baby brother alone. Or I'm telling my Daddy. I'm telling my Daddy on YOU.

Then Tatty has to shut up because first of all her voice has stopped working and because second of all she's afraid of her life in case Mam really does start smacking her instead of Luke.

But Mam isn't able to do any more smacking because all of a sudden she's sort of fainted over the side of the cot. And she stays like that just crying and crying until Jeannie brings her a basin of soapy water.

Will I do him Mam? Jeannie asks her.

Mam says no, she'll do it herself.

Mam washes Lukey and washes the cot. Washes him and kisses him, rubbing her hand over his pooey hair. She hands the basin to Jeannie so she can change the water. While she waits for Jeannie to come back with the clean water she hugs him over and over.

Lukey's elbow jumps every time Mam goes to hug him. His eyes flick back when she rubs his hair. He takes a sharp breath.

When Dad gets home he comes into the bedroom to say goodnight.

You're all very quiet tonight, he goes. What's the matter with you? Has something happened?

No. Tatty says. There's nothing the matter, we're just tired Dad that's all.

Oh well, goodnight so.

Goodnight Dad.

Jeannie whispers into the dark, Hey Tatty?

What?

I'm glad you didn't tell on Mam, I really am.

Brian whispers into the dark, Hey Tatty? I am too. I'm glad too.

If she ever does it again, I will tell on her, Tatty says. I swear. I will tell my Daddy on her. I will tell my Daddy.

You always say that, Jeannie says.

Always say what?

'My Daddy', you always say 'my Daddy', 'my Daddy'. Like he's yours and nobody else's.

1970

It's LONELY WAITING FOR MAM AND DAD TO GIVE in and start speaking again. It's lonely because nobody else in the house wants to talk, even though nobody else is having a fight. So you don't just have no one to talk to, you have no one to listen to either.

Jeannie closes the curtains in the middle of the day, gets into bed and plays with her dolls.

What's wrong with you Jeannie, why are you in bed?

I'm very sick.

No, you're *not*.

Yes, I *am*, she mimes. My asthma might be coming any minute now.

She lines the dolls up against her pillow. She whispers secrets to them and changes their clothes. If you try to join in, she ducks under the covers. Her hand comes up and pulls the dolls in. One by one, their faces go under: Sindy, Tressy, Patch, Shrimp, Linda, Barbarella.

You can hear them all whispering secrets down in the dark.

Deirdre sits on her rocking horse in front of the telly. She only wants to make her little *eee-eee* sound even though she knows buckets of words by now.

She only wants to rock on her horse even though you show her your half-a-crown that Dad gave you and say you'll bring her to the shops to buy her a bottle of *Miiiir-an-daaaa*.

She says the *eee-eee* sound soft; she makes it go with the slow rock of the horse. If you try to pull her off the horse she makes it go faster, faster, then the *eee-eee* sound gets very loud.

After a while she slides down off the horse; her eyes are dizzy while she looks for the sofa. She finds it and squeezes herself in behind. Then goes for her little sleep.

Lukey sits in his playpen and stares at the wall or else he holds onto the bars and pulls himself slowly up and down on his knees. He plops down into his quilt, stuffing his soother into his mouth, lying his head on his yellow lamb pillow.

And Mam. She just wants to be on her own, locked in her bedroom, having loads of naps.

Unless she's going out with her friend Alice or maybe Aunt Sal. In one of their cars. A red Renault for Sal that her husband bought her for after she wasn't well in hospital. A blue Fiat for Alice with a hairy gonk on a string bouncing around like a madman in the back window.

She says she's going out shopping and won't be long. But she mightn't come home for ages. When she does come home she's very tired; sometimes she even forgets to bring home the shopping. Then she has to go for another nap.

It's like everyone is too tired all the time.

Except for Brian. But he's too bold to play with, always breaking things and getting Mam into trouble with the neighbours. Always breaking things and then trying to blame it on Minty.

❧

Jeannie writes this message to Tatty. The message says Mam is drunk.

Tatty has to squish her eyes up to read Jeannie's message because it's so small. Mam is drunk, it says. Mam is drunk.

No she's not, Tatty says and starts laughing because that's such a stupid thing to say about Mam.

Mams don't get drunk Jeannie, only Dads do.

Jeannie writes it down again. Yes she is. I bet they weren't shopping at all, I bet they were in the pub. You can smell it off her and look at her face, it's all crooked.

NO she is NOT, Tatty says, and gives Jeannie's arm such a Chinese burn that she gives in and says she's only messing.

She's not drunk. She's not. She's just tired.

❧

The only time you really get to hear any talking is when Dad goes away somewhere far in an airplane. Then the aunties might come on a visit. Or sometimes Aunt Sal and Alice.

Dad always shows you where he's going on the map, teaching you the name of the place he'll be: Ascot; Cheltenham; Aintree; Newmarket. Longchamps, he says that's in Paris.

He brings home presents. Most of the presents you don't care that much about because you know they'll get lost or broken. But you care about the ones from Paris: a walky-talky dog with a waggedy tail that knows how to bark in French – *wau! wau!* A rubber doll with a freckly face and if you press her belly in she sticks out her tongue. A gold statue of the Eiffel tower. A long narrow boxful of tiny perfume bottles.

When the aunties come it's always in the daytime, on two big buses, bringing biscuits and sweets; a block of black fruitcake; a few dark plums out of Moore Street they bought on the way to catch the second bus over.

When they come they come in a crowd. A crowd of aunties and a crowd of handbags. When they come, they come to give out, first about the two-bus journey, the state of the garden, the giving Mam cheek, the not helping Mam enough with the housework.

Then they give you your sweets and send you out to play in the garden so they can start giving out about Dad.

If you want to find out what they're saying about Dad, Jeannie has to go on an earwig under the window or sneak in the back way and hide in the hall.

If Pauline comes with Aunt Winnie then she's allowed to go on the earwig with Jeannie. They never bring Tatty, because they say she's too mausey, always getting caught, bumping into things or sucking in a big *Hawwww!* out real loud when she hears something good. Jeannie and Pauline mightn't always tell her what they found out on the earwig, just to have a secret, just to leave her out. And then she has to beg and beg and give them all her sweets.

Sometimes when they do tell her, she's sorry she just didn't hold onto the sweets.

When Alice and Sal come it's only at night time. They don't bother with biscuits and sweets – they just bring bottles instead. Flat square ones wrapped in tissue paper that they take out of their handbags; or round fat bottles of tonic water they carry up in their hands. They give you a few bob and a perfumey kiss goodnight. Then they send you off to bed.

You lie in the dark and hear all the laughing. You listen to the sentences twirling round outside in the living-room. You wait for the same one to come round again, trying to guess what it means.

What's good for the goose.

Bastards. The lot of them.

One of these days.

I wouldn't mind but I always wanted to go to Paris. Always.

Then you might hear Aunt Sal crying. It's a poor substitute for a baby, she says, a fucken red ren-o. A poor substitute for a child, that's what it is.

When Aunt Sal says that, Mam and Alice join in and start crying as well.

Bastards the lot of them.

One of these days.

☙

77

Dad asks her if she's made any pals in her new school. He still calls it her new school even though she's been there since Mam took her out of the brown school after the Head Teacher was mean to Deirdre. She was going into second class then and now she's in fourth confirmation class B.

She hates the green school. Hundreds of green girls running around and a stupid green dicky-bow choking her neck all day and itchy green tights that keep driving her legs mad. And no bus. Only a walk home every day down three long roads on her own.

Dad asks her this pal question every now and then and he gets all fussy when she says no, like as if she's getting the flu, or as if she's after doing something to let him down. So this day, just to keep him happy, she pretends she's made loads of new friends. Then Dad is all delighted asking all about them, where do they live and what do their dads work at.

But then he wants to know what's all their names – ohoh.

So she says she wants to do her wees, sitting on the side of the bath thinking about where she's going to find names.

She could use the names of the girls in her class but supposing Dad meets one of their dads down in the pub or the bookies. Or Hitchcock's shop when he's buying the papers and he might say, I believe your daughter is a very good friend of our Tats, and the man might say, My daughter? Hold on she's out in the car. I'll just ask her. And then he'd come back and say, Well you must be making a mistake there because my daughter says she's never even talked to your Tats in her whole life even though she sits right in front of her in school so would you mind telling me now how they could be such good friends?

Then she'd be found out and everyone in the class would know: liar, liar, pants on fire. Again.

The only other place she can think of where you find loads of names that are already there is in books. So she pictures her book-box under her bed, then pulls names out of all the different stories and mixes them up.

She takes all the girls but leaves the boys behind because even though Dad has never been to her green school, he still might know there's no boys allowed.

She comes out of the toilet and goes back into Dad.

Well, she says, there's Dinah, Lucy-Ann, Georgina – we call her George but. And Daisy, Carlotta, Bobby – her real name's Roberta. Then there's Hilary, Belinda and let's see Marjorie and, and … that's all.

My God, Dad goes, they're very fancy names, I must say.

Oh? Well the twins have plain names.

Twins as well? TWINS! Didn't I tell you you'd make pals, didn't I tell you? And twins, if you don't mind.

Yes. Pat and Isabel O'Sullivan.

Oh that's very good indeed.

And it's nice making Daddy happy with her new friends, and it's nice for her to nearly have new friends as well. Even though they're not really real, but they're not completely makey-up either like stupid Minty because they're there already in books.

She just has to pretend to be in the book herself and tag along with them, that's all. And they're nearly as good as real friends anyway, because she can go places with them and talk to them and they talk back and include her in. Sometimes they're even better than real friends, because you don't just know what they look like and where they live: you know as well what they're thinking and how they feel about things. And a real friend mightn't tell you something like that.

But then one day Dad asks her how the twins are keeping and he asks her in front of nosy Pauline.

What twins? Pauline goes

Tatty's pals, did she not tell you about them? What's this they're called – oh that's right O'Sullivan. Marjorie is it? Marjorie and, and –

Would it be Isabel? Pauline says. Pat and Isabel?

That's it! So you do know them?

Mmm, Pauline goes with her sly little smile. I know them all right, but not to talk to.

And then she's afraid of her life in case Pauline tells on her, even though she knows Pauline isn't a tell-tale but she might tell Jeannie, and then Jeannie might start leaving books out somewhere Dad could see them or she might start reading a book with the cover up to her face: *The Twins at St Clares* or, even worse, *The O'Sullivan Twins*.

Because that's the way Jeannie is: she mightn't be a squealer either, but she always lets you know she could be if she wanted.

So all her nearly friends have to go back where they came from; back to their stories, back in their box, and she decides the next time Dad asks her about the twins she'll say they moved to Cork or else to Australia.

She misses them all the time. Misses going asleep at night and seeing them cycling beside her or waving back and calling out to her from the top of a hill – I say Tatty, do hurry along!

And going off places with them where nobody else can find you: Smugglers Top or Rilloby Fair. Moon Castle or Billycock Hill. Malory Towers, Kirrin Island, Spiggy.

I say Tatty, you are a brick!

∞

Lonely and lonely. Fed up, fed up, fed up.

Mam doesn't let anyone stay the night when she's not speaking to Dad, so that means no cousins.

Ah Mam, why?

Because I said so.

Ah please Mam, come-on. Just for the weekend. One night then *plee-eease*?

I said NO.

But why Mam? Is it because they might know you and Dad are not speaking?

No.

Oh. Well is it because Pauline heard Dad saying that thing about Uncle Richie when you were having a fight?

How dare you! I don't have to explain myself to you. I said NO, and that's an end to it. Come back here you. What did Pauline hear?

Nothin'.

What did she hear?

Don't know.

Tell me I said, now I'm warning you.

What Dad said about Uncle Richie.

What? *What?*

Oh Mam, please, I don't want to say it. I promised Pauline.

You *have* to tell me.

But you were there Mam, you know what he said.

I can't remember. I want you to tell me.

He said, he said ...

What?

There's too many curses Mam.

Just tell me.

Everything?

Everything.

So Tatty tries to remember everything: Pauline pinching her arm to wake her up – *owww!* Pauline sitting up in the bed her little white face, nervous and at the same time all excited, saying, Shhh, shhh, listen. They're fighting about uncle Richie. Oh and the curses!

How do you know about Uncle Richie? She asked Pauline. You're not supposed to –

Shut up, of course I do. Just don't tell my mam.

Dad's voice then being so mean to Mam, saying those things about her brother that Mam loved so much: You and your whole family. Fuckers the lot of them. Don't talk to me about – Don't talk to me. Denying their mother's son. Their own mother's son. Leaving him up in that place on his own. Shell-shock my arse. Rotten with the pox, more like. That he picked up in Egypt. They're so fucken respectable they can't admit it. So fucken respectable they'll leave him to rot on his own. And that's how you'll end up if you don't change your ways, in some madhouse, with your tongue hanging out. With your tongue hanging out; lalalala-la. Just like your brother. Your pox-ridden brother. Lalala-la.

That's what he said Mam. But it doesn't matter Mam, Pauline didn't believe him. Pauline said it was stupid because how could anyone spend their whole life in hospital just for having the chicken-pox? And she knew about him already Mam. She knew. But Aunt Winnie doesn't know she knows. I didn't tell her, I swear.

Shut up, Mam says. Shut up. That's enough.

Don't cry Mam. Please don't cry. I'm sorry, I am.

☙

And Dad doesn't let you stay the night in the aunties' houses when he's not speaking to Mam.

Ah Dad please, can I go?

What would you want to go over there for?

I'm bored Dad.

Haven't you Jeannie to play with?

She doesn't want to play. She has her own friends.

Well haven't you got your own friends?

They're gone to Australia.

They couldn't *all* be gone to bloody Australia.

No. But … em … they live too far away.

I see. Well read your books then.

I've read them all.

I'll give you money for new ones.

I don't want new ones. Just for the weekend. *Pleeeease.* One night then, ah go on.

Tell you what, you can come to the races with me instead.

I hate the races.

Ah how could you hate the races?

Why won't you let me go? It's not fair. Why NOT? Will you please, please just tell me why?

I will of course. It's because they're a shower of ignorant, mealy-mouthed knackers, and I don't want my children contaminated by them.

Oh. But … ?

But what?

But does that mean I can't go visiting on my confirmation day?

Of course you can. You can do whatever you like on your big confo day.

⁌

So here's her big confo day. Mam takes her on a visit to see Aunt June.

When they get there all the cousins are in school, and the cousin with the flick has got married. So there's nothing to do only stay in the kitchen and listen to Mam giving out stink about Dad. Mam is giving her a headache with all her giving out. After a while Aunt June starts making these little not-in-front-of-the-children faces, but it's like as if Mam isn't able to stop. Isn't able to stop.

Until Tatty starts crying.

She doesn't mean to cry: it just bursts out of her and then it won't go back in. It makes her head funny, too light in the inside, but too heavy to hold up. She has to lie it down on Aunt Juney's good shiny table. Nobody says anything for ages so she just leaves her head where it is, crying away, until Aunt June pulls her up by the shoulders.

Ah what's all this? she says. What's all this on your special day? Here show us your face till I give it a rub of the
flannel. What's got into you at all?

Tatty doesn't know how to explain what's got into her
at all, so she just says she has a pain in her stomach.

It's probably all the excitement, Aunt June says, isn't
that right? Of course it is. You're just overexcited about
your old confo – isn't that right?

Yes Aunt June.

Then Aunt June gives her a biscuit. You're just overexcited about your old confo that's all, she says again.

But how could you be overexcited about something you
hate – like your stupid confo? And your stupid dress-and-
coat suit with the squiggles all over like fat turquoise snails
that she heard Mam saying on the phone made her look
like a little fat granny as if she wasn't plain enough already
God bless her. And the jockey cap squashed down on your
head making your hair all sweaty. And those sling-back
shoes slipping off your heels every minute trying to make
you fall flat on your face.

And how could you be overexcited about Dad on his
own dropping you to the church and then driving away
and not coming back? And then. And then later outside
watching every single girl in fourth class getting their snaps
taken with a mam and dad each – thinking they're all great
because they're going off somewhere nice together. In their
dad's car or maybe in a taxi or it could be just standing at
the bus-stop waiting on the bus. But always with a mam and
dad and a whole family even except for Bridget Pearse whose
mam is dead but who has a blondy aunty to go round with

instead. And then hanging about on your own for ages on the empty steps of the church because everyone is gone and Mam is dead late coming in her taxi. And knowing by her face through the window of the taxi that she's in another bad humour. Then going to the hotel for lunch and seeing that man off the telly with a woman Mam said probably wasn't even his wife because they're all the same bloody men given half the chance. All the bloody –

What do you mean Mam?

I mean going off with other women.

Why?

Oh nothing, forget it.

Dad doesn't.

What? I can't hear you, you're muttering again.

I said my Dad doesn't go with other women.

How do *I* know? How do *I* know what he does or doesn't?

And then another taxi to visit Aunt June and nothing to listen to only Mam giving out all day, all day. And then bursting out crying and making a show of yourself and the stinky feel of Aunt June's flannel still on your face. Well, *how*? How could you be overexcited about THAT?

ᘓ

She starts getting holes in her hair. Brian is the first one to notice.

What's that hole in your hair? he goes.

What hole? What are you talking about?

That hole.

Don't be so stupid you. How could you have a hole in your hair?

You have, you have. Look. There.

He walks up to her, his finger pointing to the back of her head. He brings his finger nearer, is just about to touch her head, then he goes, YAAAAK! pulling his finger back real quick like as if something's after giving it a bite.

You big messer, Tatty says, picking up the little hand mirror out of the set that Aunt Winnie bought her for her confo. She tells Brian to hold the mirror behind her head the way the hairdresser does when she's showing Mam the back of her hairstyle. She looks in the dressing-table mirror. Then she sees it.

It's round and white like a little island in the middle of her head.

It's a baldy patch that all the hair must have fallen out of.

It's a little round creature with a life of its own that's been eating her hair for its dinner.

It's a big hole in her hair.

Oh Goney! Oh Goney! Oh help me! Oh Mammy! Where is it? Where is it gone?

She starts screaming around the room looking for a lump of hair that maybe she can stick back on her head. But she can't find it anywhere.

Brian's face is white and his eyes are afraid. *Tatty*, he whispers.

What? *What?*

There's another one. Another one, look. Just there.

CR

When you're the train-puller out in the yard, it means you're the engine, the most important part of the train.

All the girls have to queue up behind you, grabbing onto you, jumper by jumper. They have to wait till you're ready. They have to wait till you go *chooo! chooo!* Then the train starts to move.

She isn't the biggest train-puller in the yard, but she's the best one. Everyone fights to be on her train. Everyone calls out her name.

She can feel the weight of the girls swinging out of her jumper; she can feel the train sway behind her all over the yard. She pulls so hard her knees are down to the ground, her back is burning, the skin on her face nearly bursts open.

When the bell rings, it's time to go in again. She runs into the toilet and washes her face, stretches her back and gives it a rub. She comes into the classroom and sits in her place down the back on her own.

CR

She thinks about getting a friend. A real friend this time, not someone out of a book. But not a best friend either, because you might have to care about them too much and that would mean you'd have to fight with them and call them names and say mean things to them about their sisters and brothers. And then you'd have to hear them do the same to you.

Just an ordinary friend would do, someone to play with now and then. Walk home from school with maybe, tell them your news. Listen to them telling theirs.

But how do you get them?

She thinks about asking Jeannie and what she might say – Hey Jeannie, how do you get friends?

But Jeannie doesn't like you asking her business. Jeannie would say to her, Don't ask me my business or I'll give you such a dig.

Jeannie has lots of friends even though Mam's always saying she worries about her because she's so quiet. But when Jeannie's with her friends she doesn't seem quiet. She sees Jeannie sometimes, playing with her friends on a road that's near to their school but far from their house. Jeannie plays skipping with her friends. Or kerbs. Or piggybeds. But sometimes they don't play anything. Sometimes they just sit on the wall swinging their legs, reading the *Jackie*, laughing and talking in between.

She can't find a friend on her own road. Everyone is too small or too stupid. It's all dolls and prams and quiet little games in gardens behind gates tied together with bits of old scarves or stockings or J Cloths. And if you want to go in, the mam has to come out and open the knot with her nails. And if you don't like it when you get in there you have to call the mam back out again and she might think you don't like playing with her kids so you have to stay there because if you climb over the wall she might give out to you and say Brendan Herlihy is copying off you when he falls off the wall and bursts his lip open.

She thinks about asking Mam and what she might say – Hey Mam, how do you get friends?

You ring them up on the phone and tell them all your news. You make them tea then they tell you all their news. You give them a loan of your hats and handbags when they're going to a wedding. You go out shopping with them; you make drinks out of the bottles they take out of their handbags. You tell them your news again.

But most of Mam's friends are her sisters. Except for Aunt Sal and Alice.

When Mam goes out with Aunt Sal or Alice, she gives you money to buy the lunch. Chips if it's Friday, because the chipper is open during the day, or if it's not Friday, a tin of Queen Maeve stew and a tin of peas or maybe a tin of steak-and-kidney pie.

Just this once won't do you any harm, is what she always says.

Then Jeannie goes mad because Mam can't count. That's the third *once* this week, Jeannie goes, I mean to say, how many *onces* does she think you're allowed to have in the one week?

But Tatty doesn't mind how many onces there are in the one week.

She loves being in charge of the lunch, setting the table whatever way she likes, counting the chips out one by one, or feeling the new fancy tin opener in her hand biting its way round the tin. It takes ages to get around the steak-and-kidney pie and when you lift off the lid you see its big pasty face. Then you poke two eyes and a smile into the pie and play the records as loud as they'll go while you wait for its face to puff up brown in the oven. Dancing through the house with Lukey up in your arms, Deirdre and Brian behind you going.

Sugar – ahahah-ah-ahah – ahhoneyhoney.

Jeannie tries to catch Tatty's eye when Mam comes in the front door.

But Tatty always looks the other way.

Jeannie tries to say something to Tatty when Mam passes through the living-room.

But Tatty covers her ears. And closes her eyes. And goes into another room.

In case Jeannie tries to make her read one of her stupid messages, saying more of those stupid things about Mam.

Hey Dad, how do you get friends? She thinks about asking him and what he might say.

You go to the pub and you buy them drink. You give them a lift in your car to the races. You buy their little ticket for getting into the races; then you buy them more drink and tell them loads of jokes. If they're hungry you buy them something to eat on the way home: a big brown steak and long pale chips. And *that's* why they like you and want to be your friend.

1971

YOU GIVE THEM SOMETHING THEY LIKE.

Dad puts blobs of mustard on his beef.

Mam smooths out the bubbles on melted cheese.

Deirdre stretches her Curly Wurly with her teeth.

Brian plays Malteser marbles.

Jeannie picks the pink scabs off Brunches.

Lukey rubs Liga into his gums.

Everybody likes eating something; everybody likes touching the stuff that they eat.

Except Gemma Coughlan who can't bear the feel of anything in her mouth. Even her tongue drives her mad, always tapping at it with her finger as if she hopes it's after falling out. She gives her lunch away, usually to Bridget Pearse except when the lunch is no good. Then Bridget tells her to give it to somebody else.

Tatty is never the somebody else. But that's all right because when Bridget Pearse says Gemma's lunch is no good, it means greasy cornbeef or lumpy beetroot that makes the bread look like a bandage with the blood leaking out.

She told her cousin Pauline all about Gemma Coughlan's lunches.

Pauline said, Guess how you'll know if a girl in your class is poor?

How?

She'll be the one who'll take the lunch that Bridget Pearse won't eat.

The teacher says to Tatty, Stop daydreaming out that window.

The teacher doesn't call her Tatty, she calls her Caroline then says her surname in Irish, and that makes it sound as if it belongs to somebody else. But she isn't daydreaming out that window, she isn't even looking near it, she's looking at the long shelf underneath.

Looking at the shelf, and thinking about the lunches.

Some lunches are big and take up loads of room. They're the ones that always have treats sitting on top: lumps of fruit or chocolate snowballs, Cadbury Snacks and Fruit Pastilles. And some of the lunches are so small they hardly take up any room; you might just see one packet of Perri crisps in the corner on its own, and once there was even a half a Macaroon bar that somebody's mam had sliced straight down the middle so she could share it with her sister that's in communion class C.

If you count the lunches and count the girls and there's more girls in the classroom than lunches on the shelf, that's another good way to know if there's poor girls in your class, Pauline says. Unless they just forgot their lunch by mistake.

When somebody forgets their lunch by mistake, a mam might come knocking on the door in the middle of class. Then you have to cock your ear up to listen through the whispers.

Oh I'm sorry to *whishwhishwhish*, but would you ever *whishwhish* this to *whishwhishwhishwhish*. Thanks very *whishwhish*.

If the teacher answers you mightn't be able to see who owns the mam because the teacher's back is so big and she barely opens the door. Then you're scared stiff in case it's your Mam because you know everyone is going to stare at her out through the window when she's crossing back over the yard.

But if one of the girls answers the door you might be able to recognise a bit of the mam; her shoes or her jumper, a whirl of her hair. If you don't recognise anything that means you don't own her. Then you go *phewww* and sit up dead straight so you can look out the window and stare like mad at whoever's mam it is that's crossing back over the yard.

Looking at the shelf ...

Tupperware boxes made of pale plastic. Packages of grey greaseproof paper. Soft squares of glittery foil. Waxy sliced-pan wrapper. A bundle like you get in the butcher's that belongs to Bernie Hynes – because she's the only one who has a butcher-dad.

Tartan flasks, plastic beakers, milk in glass bottles like the milkman brings only much smaller. There's other bottles with milk in them too, bottles that used to be for something else: Milk of Magnesia say or Powers Gold Label whiskey or maybe an old cough bottle, like the one Imelda Rooney's mam forgot to wash out – pinky-white when she poured it down the sink, like melted raspberry-ripple.

Little whiskey bottles are called Baby Powers, and if there's one on the lunch shelf everyone knows it belongs to Niamh Lawlor.

A while ago you might have seen two Baby Powers on the shelf and you'd know the second one belonged to Tatty. If someone shouted out, Who owns this other little whiskey bottle? *Cé leis é?* Tatty would shout back, I do! Mine! *Is liomsa é!*

But that was before Jeannie told her how to be ashamed.

When you go to the same school as your sister, you're supposed to walk there together even if you're in different classes. But Jeannie always wants to walk on her own.

She says it's because she doesn't want Tatty to talk to her friends that she meets at the corner. She doesn't want her to talk to them in case she starts telling all the family business or worse in case she starts making up stupid stories that only somebody off their rocker would believe. Big blabber-mouth, that's what Jeannie calls her and that's why Tatty has to give her sister a five-minute start everyday.

But this day Tatty gets fed up waiting in the cold for the five minutes to be up, so she starts walking behind Jeannie after only about two. Then she sees Jeannie throw something over a wall. She thinks it's a hanky the way Jeannie just tosses it over like that, into the bushes of a house on the corner of Fernhill Road.

But when she gets to the corner and looks over there's no hanky. There's a Baby Power bottleful of milk caught in the end of the bushes. And it isn't on its own either: there's another little stack of them down by the wall. They make her think of a litter of baldy new pups snuggled in like that together, close to the wall. They make her think that's a strange thing to do, throw your milk over the wall. Even for Jeannie, it's strange.

She runs until she catches up with her sister.

What did you do that for?

Do what?

You know – throw your milk away like that. I didn't.

I saw you. I saw you and you better tell me why or –

I didn't.

All right then, I'm telling. And I'm telling as well you won't let me walk with you going to school.

I didn't want anyone to see it.

Why?

Why do you think? Jeannie said.

How should I know?

It's a whiskey bottle, stupid.

So?

Whiskey.

So? Loads of girls bring their –

No they don't.

Niamh Law –

Niamh Lawlor's dad is a drunk. Everyone knows that.

Oh.

And I don't want people to think –

Oh.

Look there's Sharon, I have to go.

But what will you do if you get thirsty?
I won't get thirsty.
You might.
I WON'T.

And thinking about the lunches ...

Sometimes you can match the girls to their lunches. The best lunches belong to the same sort of girls. Girls with lace socks and black patent shoes. Girls like Geraldine Draper. She gets a Club Milk and a bottle of Coca-Cola that she opens with her own proper opener. She gets triangle sandwiches packed into her lunch box and King crisps her Dad buys in a shop near his work. Sometimes she puts a crisp into the sandwich, with her little finger cocked up.

She has bouncy ringlets squirting out of her head and a different ribbon for every day of the year. She wears fur white mittens in winter with a fur white scarf to match. She has lovely coloured plastic covers on her schoolbooks; her pencil-case is always packed.

You couldn't give Ger Draper something she likes because she probably already has it.

Niamh Lawlor's lunch isn't a bit like Ger Draper's. It's a one-slice jam sandwich folded over and wrapped in brown paper. There's a twist at the end to stop the paper from falling off. It looks like a brown fish lying on its side.

A brown fish with a Baby Power bottle standing *right* beside it.

She has a school-bag she hugs all the way down the road because the straps are broken; she has plastic sandals she wears in the rain. You'd think you could give Niamh

Lawlor something she likes because she doesn't have anything to like of her own. But Niamh Lawlor hates taking things. Niamh Lawlor would go mental if you tried to even give her one measly little crisp.

Tatty knows because one time she tried it, holding the bag of crisps open under Niamh's nose. You could see Niamh was really hungry for the crisps, her throat gulping, her eyes nearly popping out of her head. But she kept on saying no thanks and no thanks and no thanks. And then she lost her temper: I said NO, I said. Are you thick or just deaf?

And another time the teacher gave Niamh a catechism so she could learn all the answers for her confirmation day. The teacher said she could have it for keeps because it was only taking up room in the *cófra* and might as well be put to some use.

Niamh's face was boiling when she went up to the teacher's desk to pick up the book, boiling all over right down to her neck. You could see the book shaking in her hand when she took it back to her place. You could see her eyes rolling around with trying to squeeze back the tears, and you knew it wasn't because she was happy getting a free catechism or even embarrassed or anything like that. It was because she was raging with the teacher for making her take the book. She really hated the teacher for that.

Bridget Pearse is the opposite to Niamh. She doesn't mind taking things at all – she loves it. And she doesn't really even have to ask: people just seem to give her things all the time, or else they lend her stuff that they end up saying she can have for keeps. Even though Bridget Pearse has no mam she still gets good enough lunches, and she has plenty of nice stuff of her own. But she still wants what everybody else has; she still wants whatever she sees.

She stands at a desk and says, Oh God that's *gorgeous*!

She stands at the lunch shelf and says, Oh my favourite, you LUCKY duck.

She stands in the yard and sighs, Ahhh it's well for you …

She stands everywhere and squeals, For keeps? Are you sure? Oh thanks a million. Thanks a million, billion, trillion, ZILLION!

Rubbers so fancy they look like sweets; brand new hairslides and a stretchy Alice-band. A suck of an icepop on the way home from school that turns into a bite, that turns into the whole ice-pop. A loan of a transistor for the weekend. A comic that hasn't even been read.

That's why you could give Bridget Pearse something she likes, because she likes everything she sees (except for cornbeef or beetroot sandwiches). And even if she didn't like it that much you know she'd probably still take it. And if she'd take it, she might be your friend.

And if she was your friend, that would chuck Jeannie. And Mam. And Dad. And Deirdre. And Brian and his stupid Minty as well.

CR

Mam says Tatty has to go to the butcher's: a pounda mince, a halfa pounda rib.

She has to make sure to put the change right down in her pocket so she won't lose it, because Mam only has one note until she goes to the bank.

Mam says she'll write the messages down in case Tatty forgets, but then she can't find any biro.

A pounda mince.

The bank is in Terenure so she has to hurry because that means they have to get the bus and they might be waiting for ages. After the bank they have to buy new shoes for Deirdre in Cripps.

A halfa pounda rib.

And that's why Mam wants to put the dinner on, so it'll be ready for when they get back.

A pounda?

Mince, rib. Rib, mince.

A big fat pound of one, a little half-pound of the other.

When they're down in Terenure, they might go into Eaton's and then Mam might buy them a chocolate bunny-biscuit for after if they eat their dinner. When they're down in Terenure, she might see if Mam is still in a bad humour from not speaking to Dad. If she's not in bad humour she might ask can they go into Copeland's to look at the books.

Copeland's has books in long rows that go all the way down into the dark. O'Connor's only has a few on a stand. Stupid Ladybird books about Peter and Jane and only a few other good ones that you always finish ages before they get new ones in again.

Deirdre doesn't like Ladybird books; she's afraid of Peter and Jane. When you show her their picture she screams and puts her face in the cushion. Mam says she wouldn't blame her either because they look too peculiar. They look like an oulone and oulfella dressed up as kids.

The books at the top of the stand are all about kissing. But you're not allowed look at them. You can only see them properly if you stay at the door and go up on your tippy-toes, letting on to look at the boxes of Daz and the tins of sardines on the shelf behind.

Sometimes it's a doctor kissing a nurse, or it might be a pilot kissing an air hostess, or a boss kissing the lady who does the typing – but there's always somebody kissing someone.

Mam does Dad's typing.

Clickclickclickclatterclick. PING!

He carries the typewriter into the kitchen and puts it on the table, pushing all the breakfast things out of the way with his elbows. He stands behind her and tells her what to type. She can go as fast as his voice. First the page is stiff and straight but then it starts to bend. First the page is bare as snow. Then it starts to fill up with black-word hedges.

If they're not speaking Dad writes out the letter and leaves it on the kitchen table for Mam to copy off. Mam puts all the breakfast things away one by one and wipes the table down. Then she carries the typewriter in on her own.

When O'Connor's put new books on the stand you can see if you can get away with playing your trick. Here's how you play your trick. You buy a book, read it real quick, then bring it back and say, I didn't know my sister already has this book, so can I change it for another one please?

You have to make sure you don't leave any marks on the book though, you couldn't eat crisps or turn down the pages. You have to make sure Mr O'Connor is behind the counter, because he always lets you away with it.

Mrs O'Connor wouldn't though, she'd say, I'm sorry that's simply out of the question! What do you think this is – a liba-rare-ree?

The woman who helps Mrs O'Connor wouldn't fall for the trick either. She'd say, Would ya get away outa that, or I'll give you such a kick up the you-know-what. Go on now off with yourself before I tell your mother.

The woman who works there is called Ava. She has a squashy nose. She sounds like she has a cold. When she speaks you have to listen carefully or you might think she's saying brother instead of mother. Then you might wonder why she's going to tell Brian.

A bounda bince and a halfa bounda wib.

But when Tatty gets to the butcher's shop, she passes right by. Then crosses the road and passes right by in the opposite direction.

She counts the reasons for not going in.

The boss is in there and he always jeers her. He says, Are you still sucking that oul thumb of yours? Go on then, give us a suck.

The shop is full of a horrible smell and when the door closes behind you can't breathe properly because every time you open your mouth the smell squeezes in through your teeth.

The mince looks like a hill of sore worms. The sausages look like dead fingers.

The boss-butcher always calls her Ginger then says he's going to marry her, wiping the side of his knife on his apron all damp with blood.

Once he showed her a red slimy heart and told her it was the heart of a little girl who wouldn't do what she was told.

She's just remembered Bridget Pearse lives round the corner.

But Bridget doesn't open the door. Her dad in his vest does instead; a mug of tea, a cigarette, a paper tucked under his elbow. There's a little head of orange hair growing out of each of his shoulders. There's a picture of a mermaid like a big blue transfer drawn down the front of one of his arms. You can see her bare boozies sticking out. That makes her shy; wanting to laugh; wanting to run away. That makes her not know what to say.

Are you looking for Bridget? Mr Pearse asks.

Eh ...

Wha'?

Eh ...

He puts his chin back over his hairy shoulder and the big roar that comes out goes: BEEZY!

Beezy. He calls her *Beezy*. That's the funniest name she ever heard in her life.

Bridget's face comes over the banister, then her feet come down the stairs slow.

What do you want?

Oh hi Bridget, I was just ...

What?

I was just ... Are you coming out?

For wha'?

Just for ... well, nothing really. Seeya.

Yeah, seeya, Bridget says and starts closing the door.

Oh Bridget wait a minute. I just remembered ... em ... you know my aunty in America? No.

Well, my aunty in America sent this to me. I couldn't think what to do with it so I was going to buy a feast. Do you want – ?

Hold on a minute. I just have to tell me – DA … ?

Wha'?

I'm going out.

Leave the door on the latch for your Aunt Pearl in case she forgets her key. And here?

What?

How long will you be?

Don't know.

Take as long as you like – no hurry back. Say an hour and a half anyway at least, Beezy, all right?

Beezy. He calls her *Beezy*.

Inside Hitchcock's sweetshop Tatty tries to keep everything nice and slow.

Mr Hitchcock taps his fingers on the counter; she studies the shelves behind him, row after row after row. Mr Hitchcock has his hand ready at the penny jars and halfpenny boxes. She leans into the glass over the fresh-cream-cake display. Mr Hitchcock gives a fed-up sigh and asks if she's made up her mind.

Nearly, em, just another minute, em …

Well don't keep us in suspense, he says, whatever you do.

Then he walks to the other end of the counter and starts fiddling with his newspaper spread.

Excuse me, Mister Hitchcock?

Hah?

I'm ready now.

He comes back and stands by the penny jars.

She fills up her lungs: Aaaaaa ... bagofmarshmallowsalargebottleofraspberrytwobarsoftif fentwobarsofrumandbuttertwoturkishdelightandatoble rone – do you like Toblerones Bridget?

Oh Toblerones! They're my *very* favourite.

Two Toblerones and –

Crisps, Bridget says, don't forget the crisps.

Oh yeah. Two packets of cheese and onion.

Salt and vinegar, Bridget says.

Oh, I mean two packets of salt and –

No. As well. Get them as *well*.

Right, two bags of each please. And –

Fry's Cream

Two bars of Fry's Cream and ... she looks at Bridget to see what else.

Milk Tray, Bridget says.

A bag of Milk Tray.

What about Walnut Whips? Do you like Walnut Whips Caroline? I love Walnut Whips.

Begod, Mr Hitchcock says, youse'll be a right pair of fatsos by the time ye've done with that lot. Did somebody win the pools?

No, Tatty says. No. I ... em ... We ... eh ... Actually, Bridget says, her aunty sent her money from America.

You've an aunty in America? Oh now. Which part?

Oh Goney, what do you call the name of that place again?

Hollywood, Bridget says. Here, we nearly forgot the cream cakes, and do you think it would it be all right if I got a comic as well Caroline?

Yeah, Tatty says, you can have anything you want.

Sure?

Yeah.
Really?
Really.
Oh thanks a million, billion, trillion, ZILLION!

They go up to Cullen's field behind the new houses. Tatty spreads out the feast between them; Bridget sits like an Indian, resting the *June and Schoolfriend* on the triangles she's made with her legs. Then she gets stuck into the bag of marshmallows.

When she wants a drink she stretches her hand out to the bottle of raspberry and Tatty passes it over. Here's what Bridget does next. She rubs the palm of her hand down hard on the top of the bottle, then shoves it into her mouth. She flicks her head back, starts swigging like mad, then hundreds of googoos come flying out of her mouth and go twirling around in the raspberry. She pulls the bottle away and gives it another rub.

Wanna slug? she asks and out comes a long scrawny belch.

No thanks.

She passes the bottle back, pulls the next thing out of the feast and goes back to reading her comic. Sometimes she lies back in the grass and holds the comic open over her head. Then you can see right into her mouth.

Bridget eats with her mouth wide open but she doesn't really speak because she's too busy reading and anyway her mouth is too full of thick pink marshmallow and sharp bits of crisps and blobs of black chocolate tumbling around.

It's a bit like doing your ecker, trying to think of inter-esting sentences to say to Bridget Pearse, something to make her look up from her comic. And all Bridget does is go – Mmm, mmm, yeah yeah, mmm. Or else she might not bother answering at all, just give a bit of a shrug.

Would you like to live in one of those new houses Bridget?

Shrug.

Do you ever watch *The Fugitive*, Bridget?

Mmm.

Do you think they'll ever catch him?

Maybe.

What do you think of fifth class Bridget? Do you think it's any good?

Shrug.

I think it's all right. It's better than fourth class anyway – what are you getting for Christmas?

Don't know.

I thought your confirmation outfit was lovely.

Mmm.

The nicest in the class, I thought it was.

Yeah.

Tatty stares into Bridget's wide-open mouth and thinks about Alice's new washing-machine, in a special room that they have in their house just for the clothes, all folded on shelves, and a fancy ironing-board that fits into a press and the roundy window on the front of the washing-machine, all the different colours going up and down and …

Then Bridget says something!

Sorry Bridget?

I said, did you ever see me Aunty Pearl?

Not really, just at the church on confirmation day. She looks nice.

She's all right I suppose. She's not me real aunty but.

Well who is she then?

Don't know, but look, she gave me this ring.

Oh that's lovely.

And this cross and chain.

Oh yeah.

She's always giving me things.

Is she?

Yeah, she even gave me this pink cardigan – is there any raspberry left?

No, it's all gone.

I knew we should have gettin' two bottles.

I still have some money left, will we go back down to Hitch – ?

Nah. It's all right, I'm stuffed now in anyway, and I'm freezing.

Do you want my coat?

Nah I think I'll just go home.

Home?

Yeah – here are you not eating that Toblerone?

Then Tatty starts getting a pain in her belly from all the rubbish squashed up inside. And from thinking about everyone waiting in the hall. Faces all washed, hairs all combed, coats buttoned up to the neck. Deirdre with the whitest socks out of the sock box for trying on her new shoes in Cripps. Brian in his good short pants, holding onto the go-car handle with Lukey in his pull-ups sitting inside. Jeannie standing dead straight in the corner. The onions and carrots peeled on the draining board, waiting on the meat so they can be a stew. Mam looking out the window every few minutes, then going out to the gate, leaning over, taking a long look up the road.

Her step getting quicker each time, her hands getting jumpy, the way they always do when her temper is coming. And her face getting redder and redder and …

Will you come home with me Bridget?

For what?

To tell my Mam – I mean.

To tell your Mam what?

I think I might be in trouble.

Why?

I just might be.

Here – you didn't steal that money, did you?

NO, I did *not*. But …

But what?

I wasn't supposed to spend it, so I might just say I lost it on the road and I called for you to help me look for it. Please. I'll give you all the change that's left over. *Please.*

Ahh, I don't feel like it, I'm jacked.

Please.

Ah no, I don't want to.

Please. I'm begging you, Bridget, I'm begging. And I won't tell anyone your Dad calls you Beezy.

You shut up, he does not.

Oh I know he doesn't. I'm just saying in case he ever does, I wouldn't tell anyone anyway.

You shut up. Or I'll give you that. Do you hear me? THAT!

Bridget's fist comes up to her face, gives two little shakes, then swings away and goes off in a huff with the rest of her. Leaving Tatty all on her own.

Tatty all on her own. Wants to cry. Or run across the road real quick, get knocked down, die. Or maybe just get kidnapped instead; except if a dangerous stranger offered her sweets now she'd be too stuffed to take them. Or she could always faint and crack her head on the ground then she wouldn't be able to remember who she was, what happened to the meat money or even the meat. But then Bridget walks back again.

She better not start giving out to me, she says, because I can't stand people's mothers giving out.

Oh no. She never gives out. She's real soft.

Well what are you so afraid of then?

I don't know.

All right then, Bridget sighs, holding out her hand for the change. Tell us what I've to say again.

But it doesn't matter what she has to say again, and it doesn't matter how many times they practise it on the corner before they go in. Because Bridget isn't going to say it anyway and Mam isn't going to listen. She opens the door, her hand comes out, drags Tatty in.

Where were you? Where WE-EEE-RE you?

Then she sees Bridget: Who's that youngone? Who are you?

Me-ee? I'm in her class.

What are you doing here?

Me-ee? Well she called for me so she did, because she had money her aunty sent from America.

WHAT? ·

Her aunty and she asked me if I wanted ... Bridget says walking backwards away from the door.

What did you do with the money?

Me-ee? I didn't touch it. She spent it in Hitchcock's. It wasn't my fault. She told me. Her aunty. She told me. I swear. It wasn't. I didn't. On the holy bible. You can even ask my Da, if you like because my Ma is –

What's your name?

Bridget.

Well Bridget, if you take my advice, you'll have nothing more to do with her, do you hear me? Nothing. She's a pathological liar. A path-ol –

A *wha*?

Go HOME.

Mam slams the door in Bridget Pearse's face.

Before Mam slams the door, Tatty can see Bridget Pearse's pink cardigan sliding backwards down the drive. After Mam slams the door, she can see it through the bumpy glass. It breaks up into little pink bubbles. It shoots through every window in the porch: one, two, three, four. Then it melts away.

I'm sorry Mam, she says. I'm really sorry, I'll never do it again. I swear.

But Mam doesn't care if she's sorry or not.

Mam drags her by the hair across the living-room. My hair Mam, mind my hair, you'll make it fall out. My hair.

Mam lets go of her hair and flings her on the floor. The floor gives her a big slap in the stomach. That makes her ears go fizzy and fill up with echoes, but she can still hear Mam's voice shouting.

Not everything Mam says makes sense: there's lot's of cursing that Pauline would just love; other stuff she can't understand – gobbledegook Mam is talking. Gobbledegook.

But the names Mam calls her are clear enough.

Liar. Bitch. How dare you? Ugly little. Liar bitch. Liar just like that bastard, ugly. Little Bitch. I'm going to kill you, do you hear me? Kill you.

Tatty believes Mam when she says that. Because just then she can feel the air go out of her. *Foo-oosh!* And it makes her think of when you blow up an empty bag then put it on the ground and stamp on it real quick. *Foo-oosh!*

And she tries to say, My back Mam, my back. You're hurting it too much Mam. You're stamping on my back.

But her voice won't work because the air is gone out of her.

And Mam is still shouting so loud she probably wouldn't be able to hear her anyway. But then she finds out that she's been wrong about Mam stamping on her back. It isn't Mam at all! It's the sweeping brush. Mam is hitting her with the sweeping brush across her back. Holding it wide in her arms, lifting it up, then bashing it down. Her knee is stuck into Tatty's bum but she isn't stamping on her. Her Mam isn't stamping on her. It's the sweeping brush. That's what it is. The sweeping.

The room feels so big around her. Big as the assembly-hall in school. She tries to listen past Mam's voice, to see if anyone is going to stick up for her. If anyone is going to say, You leave her alone, you leave her alone. Or I'm telling my Daddy on you. I'm telling my Daddy.

But there's nothing. Only the grunts of Deirdre trying to squeeze in behind the sofa. The sniffs of Brian in a faraway corner. The sound of a door softly closing. And Mam.

Liar. Bitch. Liar. Ugly.

Mam.

Bloody. Little.
Mam, I think I'm –
Ugly.
Mam, I'm going to get –
Ugly. Little. Liar.
Mam, sick. Sick. Mammy. Sick.

ᄋᎡ

Oh when will the second big fight ever come? Oh when will it make them be friends again?

Jeannie says there's no point in waiting for it anymore because the breaks between fights are getting so short it means the next first fight comes around too soon, and then you don't know if that counts as the third or the first fight, and in anyway as far as she can see the last few second fights didn't make all that much difference.

So you're better off not even counting, Jeannie says. You're better off finding a dark spot: a corner somewhere or under the covers if it's in the middle of the night. Then covering your ears with a pillow. Shut your eyes tight. Start cursing your head off.

Cursing?

Yeah. Cursing and cursing, the worst ones that you've ever heard in your whole life – in a pub maybe somewhere or off a dirty drunk at the races. And if you rock your head from side to side, holding the pillow steady, all the curses will slide up and down in your head, filling it up to the brim, right out to the holes in your ears. And then no sounds will get in. No sounds; no voices; no fights – so who cares then and what difference which number fight it is?

But Tatty still wants to wait for the second big fight; for the smell and the sound of it, the way that it moves, the shape that it has. Tatty still waits.

It doesn't have to happen in the middle of the night either, not like the first big fight, it can happen any time it wants. Sometimes you know it's coming because you feel it getting nearer, nearer, NEARER.

But other times it comes as a surprise.

Say if Dad is helping Tatty with her homework. And he puts his hand down flat on the table, leaning over her shoulder. She picks out his smells: onion, porter, peppermint, mustard, all mixed up in the warm little ball of his breath.

Then he starts teaching her how to make points.

Dad thinks everyone should know how to make points because you can use them for all sorts of things, not just your ecker. They're a way to make people listen to you, to understand exactly what it is you're trying to say.

Do you get me? he asks.

Kind of …

All right. Now. Supposin' the teacher gives you a question about a poem or a story. Then instead of arsing around the page tripping over ideas, you just think hard about what the question is *really* asking you, then you read it again and catch the bits that jump out at you. After that, all you have to do is write down something like, In my opinion this poem can be summarised as follows: a) *blablablabla* – the first bit that jumps out; and b) *blablablabla* – the second bit. And so on and so on, till nothing else jumps out and that's when you know you've all your points covered.

The *blablablabla* bit sounds funny when he says it, but summarise sounds warm and roundy. Dad shows her how to put the belly bracket around the 'a' and the 'b'.

It's called alphabetising, he says.

Alpha – like the … ?

Good girl, yes. Good girl. Like the alphabet, *exactly*.

Al-pha-bet-ising.

And that sounds nice as well.

But Mam doesn't think it sounds nice, shuffling around the kitchenette, making herself a cup of tea after being out in town buying the clothes for Christmas. Mam thinks it sounds bloody ridiculous. Her voice pops out of the kitchenette – Bloody ridiculous, it says, bloody ridiculous. Hah!

Dad lifts his head for a second, then lowers it again.

We'll ignore her now, he says to Tatty out the side of his mouth. We'll ignore her – right?

But then another little laugh comes out of the kitchenette and up goes his head again.

Have you got something to say in there? he shouts. Have you? Have you? Because if you have, you can come out here and say it, instead of heckling like a rat out a hole.

Mam comes out from the kitchenette and leans against the wall with her coat hanging open and her good high-heels on. If I am like a rat in a hole – who put me there? WHO? Living in this hovel while you drink and gamble for Ireland. Living in this –

Oh now, you don't do too bad at all in the drink stakes yourself, Dad goes. Oh no-oh, you've nothing to be ashamed of in *that* department let me tell you sweetheart.

Ah what are you on about now?

Well one thing's for certain – you didn't get that glitter in your eye walking around Clerys looking for bargains.

Mam slips her scarf off her head, flicks it out and stuffs it into her pocket. Her face is brown with makeup and her lips are pinky-red; she's wearing a new black jumper. She shakes her hair and her eyes give a long slow blink like as if she's a doll.

You're a scream really, she says, the nonsense you come out with. And the way you talk to that child. A bloody howl!

She puts her two arms straight out behind her and her coat slips down to her wrists. Dad doesn't seem able to think of anything to say. He just keeps staring and staring at her new black jumper with his gob hanging open.

She drops her coat on the sofa and goes back to leaning against the wall. One hand on her hip, the other hand waving in the air, her eyes are flashing all over the place; she looks the way she does when she's singing a song.

I mean – I never heard the likes of it in all my life, she goes, with your al-pha-bet-ising. Hah! As if the teacher won't guess it was you. I mean, do you think she's some sort of a fool? But of course you do, you think everyone's a fool except yourself – but to actually imagine that the teacher is going to believe –

Tatty edges her bum to the side of the chair, slides it off and moves behind Dad. Softly, softly she walks to the door that leads into the hall. She pulls down the handle, sneaky, sneaky, opens it towards her, dips behind it then out to the hall. She closes the door behind her.

A child of nine! A child of nine! You expect the teacher to believe would know a word like 'summarise': that just makes me laugh that just makes me –

You don't think she'd know a word like summarise?
Dad says.

Pa-thetic, Mam says.

You don't think so?

NO.

Well, ask her then. AAAASK her – why don't you?
Because she knows it now. She fuckenwell knows it NOW.

Dingalingaling. It's time for the second big fight.

 こ

Flowers. Town. Clothes. Spree! Spree! Spree! New shoes,
new bag, new coat, new suit, new dress, new slip, new hat.

Who's going to mind us when you go to the races Mam?

I'm not going to any races.

But Dad always brings you to the races when
you get new clothes. Are you going away for the weekend instead?

I'm not going anywhere.

Ah Mam – what's wrong?

Nothing, I've something stuck in my eye, that's all.
Listen do you remember a few weeks ago you stole the
meat money?

Yes Mam, I'm sorry.

You didn't say anything to your Dad by any chance?

No Mam – why? Did you? Did you tell on me?

No. Will you calm down for God's sake? I was just
wondering, that's all.

I didn't tell Mam, I swear I didn't.

Well neither did I, Mam says.

So how come Dad found out?

The reason she knows Dad found out can be summarised as follows: a) he's not talking to Mam again so soon after the last fight is over; b) he starts bringing Tatty everywhere with him, looking at her funny out the side of his eyes; c) he keeps asking her if she's all right; d) he wants to send her away.

Please don't send me away Dad, I'll be good in future, I swear I will. Please.

He's sitting on the end of the bed talking to her like a dad off the telly. He's even knocked on the door first and asked her if he could come in.

He says, Nobody is punishing you. I'm doing you a favour, if only you knew.

But Dad …

Look, it's just a school, that's all. The only difference is you sleep there. A boarding-school, it's called. Like, like one of those books you're always reading, what do you call that place again?

Malory Towers?

That's right, Malory Towers. Will you stop crying there's a good girl. You know your old Dad only wants what's best for you. Hundreds of girls would love to be given the chance to go, and let's face it you're not very happy in that oul school you're in now.

Was it something bold I did on Mam?

No. I told you, it's nothing like that.

Anyway Mam mightn't let me go. She wouldn't let Deirdre go when –

It's not up to Mam and it's a different thing alto-gether. You'll make loads of friends, have your own little room and you'll be able to go horse-riding and play tennis and –

How do you know I'll make friends?

Because you'll all be living together, like sisters.

But sometimes sisters don't even like each other.

True. But there'll be hundreds of girls there: stands to reason you'll have to make friends with one or two of them.

When would I have to go?

The sooner the better. You'll be ten in a few days – you could go after that.

But fifth class has already started Dad. The first term is nearly over and all.

I know. But that wouldn't matter, you could always go in late.

Would they not mind?

No. Of course they wouldn't mind. So what do you say?

I don't know, what do you say Dad?

I want you to do whatever you want.

But I don't know whatever I want.

All right. Fair enough. Think about it. And let me know.

He stands up and pats the bed like a dog.

CR

The next thing Mam is pregnant. Tatty finds out the day of her birthday, a few days before she's to start her new school. She reads it in one of the notes on the kitchen table. The notes are for when they're not speaking. Mam's ones to Dad are usually about phone messages or else they're to ask him for money. Dad's ones to Mam are usually about something she has to type or else they're to tell her what to say if someone rings up. Usually means nearly all the time.

Dad's writing is long and narrow and leans forward. Mam's writing is roundy and short, it leans the other way.

I'm pregnant again, it says. I hope you're satisfied now. I hope you're bloody happy now.

ଓଥ

Crispy tissue all over the bed, shiny cardboard boxes, carrier bags with shop names on the side. She's never owned so much stuff in her life. It makes her feel like someone off the pictures or like Mam after one of her sprees.

Dad says it's like loading Noah's Ark trying to get her packed, with her two of this and her two of that: tick, tick, tick, tick off the list.

Then he says he'll be back in an hour to drive her to her new school.

Mam comes in as Dad goes out. The telephone rings in Dad's bedroom; she can hear his steps go towards it.

For a while Mam stays quiet in the middle of the room just looking around at all the stuff. Her hand stretches out now and then as if it's thinking about touching something. Then it flies up suddenly and snatches the list out of Tatty's hand.

Give me that bloody thing!

And first she's just muttering away to herself, giving out that Dad's bought all the wrong things, the next minute she's losing her temper, picking on the gaberdine coat first and throwing it against the wall.

A rag, that's what it is! A bloody rag, that's all. And would you look at these wellies? *Silver* for Jeee-sus sake. You'll be the laughing stock as if you're not bad enough on your own. And what's this supposed to be?

My wash-bag Mam.

Your wash-bag? Your wash-bag? Would you mind telling me how all THIS stuff is going to fit into THAT fecky little thing. You stupid thick.

Bounce go the wellies off the wall; *slap* goes the wash-bag off Tatty's arm.

Jesus Mary and Joseph, I just don't believe it. Where did you get this? she shouts, pulling the purse out of the pile on the bed.

Arnotts, it's for my pocket money, it's on the list.

Who picked this out?

Me. Dad said I could.

Oh I'm sure he did all right.

Mam opens the purse and lifts out the price tag.

Christ almighty! There's people earn less than this in a week. A WHOLE week. I wouldn't mind but it'll be lost in a day. What sort are you? What sort?

I don't know Mam.

It's disgusting that's what it is. Disgusting!

Whizz goes the purse across the room; *clip!* when it hits the wardrobe.

Oh Mammy please.

Don't you ohmammyplease ME! And look at this case. You can't even pack properly, stuffing everything in any old way at all. Do you not even know how to fold things? Oh I can see you all right managing on your own. I can just about see it!

She flips the case over, spilling the clothes all over the floor. Then she goes back to the gaberdine coat, picking it up off the floor, lashing it into Tatty's face. The belt swings out and the buckle swipes the side of her jaw.

Owww, that hurt me. That really –

Then suddenly Mam just stops.

The next thing is she's down on her knees, grabbing Tatty into this hug that makes her not be able to breathe or to move with her arms pinned down to her sides.

My baby, Mam sobs, he's taking my baby away. Taking my baby.

Tatty doesn't know what to do then, trying to think which is worse, which is more scary – Mam losing her temper, firing things all over the room, or the feel of the hug so tight and the feel of Mam crying all over her.

She stares at the wall and waits to see what will happen next.

The telephone gives a little ding and Dad's footsteps come back out.

Then Mam starts screaming out at him. Lousy bastard! That's all you are. Lousy bloody bastard!

Dad's footsteps keep moving towards the livingroom. The living-room door slams behind him.

Mam gets to her feet to run out after him.

She keeps on screaming the same thing. Through the house and into the hall, out to the front door and after his car as it pulls out of the drive. Lousy bastard! Lousy bloody bastard!

She waits for a while to see if Mam will come back. But that doesn't happen so she goes out to the back garden and asks Jeannie to give her a hand instead. Jeannie's sitting on the rusty swing, picking at her warts with the tip of her compass. The garden is icy, the high grass dripping with frost and Jeannie's bare feet are purple with the cold.

Where's your shoes Jeannie?

In the house.

Why?

I didn't want her to hear me sneaking out.

You'll get sick.

Jeannie sucks the blood out of a wart. Good, she says.

She pushes her legs into the ground and lets the swing take her up, brushing her bare feet through the long frosty grass, hanging her head back so you can't see her face.

Please Jeannie – will you help me pack?

Do it yourself *bigmouth*!

What are you calling me that for?

Big blabbermouth, I bet you told him yourself.

I didn't. I swear I didn't. Anyway what would I tell him for? I'd only get in trouble for stealing the meat money.

I bet you did. I bet you made sure he saw the marks on your back.

I did NOT.

And I don't blame Mam for giving you a hiding either. It was your own fault. Your own big fat fault. But you still shouldn't have told on her.

I didn't tell on her, I didn't.

Big trouble-maker, tell-tale-tattler, greedyfatbitch. You and that stupid Bridget Pearse. I hate the two of you. I hate YOU the most.

I'm not listening to you.

Jeannie stops swinging then; her head comes up and she drops her feet. She looks Tatty up and down.

What?

God that uniform looks dead stupid on you. You look like a –

A what?

A big blue blob. It's horrible, God it's disgusting, it's making me feel sick just looking at it.

I'm not listening, I said.

I bet it's not like Malory Towers at all. I bet it's a prison for liars and robbers. An Artane for girls, that's what it'll be.

It will not! It will not!

In anyway Dad's only sending you because he wants to get rid of you because you're such a big troublemaker blabbermouth bitch. Everyone knows the only reason parents send their children to boarding-school is because they're not wanted. And do you know what? I'm glad you're going. I hope you never come back. I hope I never ever see you again. Do you know what else I hope?

What?

I hope –

You hope what?

But Jeannie can't say what else she hopes because now she's started crying, her long whirly hair all over her face. And that seems so strange to see Jeannie crying because she never cries except when her warts just won't go away.

Jeannie? Jeannie what?

Don't.

Don't what?

Don't leave me here.

Ask Dad can you come with me.

I did ask him.

And?

No. He said, no. Because I might get sick and the nuns wouldn't be able …

Oh Jeannie I'm sorry.

Don't leave me. Not on my own. Not here. On my own.

CR

Here's how Mam fell in love with Dad. She met him at a dance at a seaside place miles away. She only got up with him for a bet from her friends because he looked sort of old-fashioned. He drove her home in his big black car. She was a bit shy of him at first because he was much older and she didn't really know what to be saying. But that didn't really matter because Dad did all the talking anyway. When they got to her house she had no light for her cigarette. Dad couldn't find his lighter. So he got out of the car and pulled up the bonnet. Then he tugged two wires out of the engine and struck them together. He ducked his head down and lit the cigarette with the spark that they made. Mam thought this was the cleverest thing she'd ever seen anyone do. Inventive was the word she used. Inventive.

Here's how Dad fell in love with Mam. He had gone out a few times with her and thought she was nice. Then one day he saw her when he wasn't expecting to, driving along in his car. He was tired from working too hard and being up late playing cards. He had a pain in his head from drinking too much whiskey the night before and from not being able to back a winner all week. The trees were bare and the street was grey. He saw her and she was wearing a yellow dress.

1972

WHEN YOU'RE IN SCHOOL, YOU THINK ABOUT HOME. The way the light from the fire jumps all over the wall in the winter. Or lying on your belly watching the telly, and waiting for the smells to come creeping out of the kitchen. Saying – That's the lamb, and there's the roast spuds, that's the brussellers now, the mushy green peas; and soon the *ahhhhh* Bisto that will cover it over. Turning everything brown and shiny and yum.

In school, there's no telly. And you never really know what you're getting for dinner until you're nearly at the top of the queue. Unless if it's chips, then you'll hear the chipswhisper whizzing back down the line.

And it always smells the same in the corridors so there's no point in sniffing for clues. Polish and potatoes. Dettol and something that smells sort of cheesy. Except for Friday when you get the fishpong. And you know that you're getting fish for dinner; and you know what it's going to be like – orange, scabby, bent hard in the middle.

But that makes it better for slipping into your pocket or into a hanky stuffed up your sleeve – so the big girls told her.

When a big girl hides a fish up her sleeve you feel so afraid for her in case she gets caught in the act or, worse even, later on flushing it down the toilet or trying to feed it to the cat who never eats it either but who sometimes carries it off in his mouth like he's going to keep it for later.

After the fish there'll be stewed-apple and custard she wouldn't have minded trying the first day, except a girl at her table told her it was all full of spits from someone who works in the kitchen called Lydia the dribbly lady.

If you work in the kitchen or wash the floors, then you're called a Domestic. Unless you're a nun: then you're called Sister, but you won't look the same as the other nuns. You'll have strings tied around the top of your arms for holding up your sleeves and a long apron tucked into your habit. You'll have hands that are scaldy with bumps.

The hands on the nuns in charge are always waxy and white.

At home you don't mind being hungry because you know it will only be a little while before your mouth will be full of Mam's juicy cooking, making you feel all cosy inside. But in school you do mind. Because you're always hungry and you always will be for the rest of the day. Unless it's the day you go mental at the Mission Drive, stuffing yourself with pink popcorn and marshmallow mice. The feel of the hot watery sick then for ages, squeezing up from your throat, leaking into your mouth.

Or unless it's a Sunday and you eat, all to yourself, a whole sliced pan and butter for tea.

You hold out your plate and your dinner comes up at you from these big silver boats bobbing around in hot greasy water. Slop, slop, slop from a big silver spoon. And even if you feel like eating it because you're so hungry, you can't because the other girls at your table might say, Ugggh, don't tell me you're going to eat *that*.

The room where you eat your dinner is called a refectory.

At home you only have to think about a few little rooms and the few little seconds it takes to get from one to the other. And no stairs. But in school you have to think about so many rooms; whereabouts they all are, how long it's going to take you to get to the next one and all the mad names they're called. And hundreds of different stairs.

Some of the names she knows already because she read it in Malory Towers. Like the room where you sleep is called a dormitory.

Except if you speak French then you have to sleep in a place called the poodle-rooms.

The Spanish girls can't have their own dorm but. They have to be mixed up with everyone else because they just can't stop talking. Then they don't learn any English. The Spanish girls are the queerest in the school. They kiss their thumbs when they're blessing themselves; they wear fancy black veils in mass. When you hear them talking together they sound like ducks that are quacking too fast. They never share their jars of chocolate stuff that they spread on their bread like black butter.

There's a studio where you paint pictures. And the artist nun shows you how to paint trees. But she says before you can paint the trees you have to get to know them. Down in the Phoenix Park. She gets you to rub their wrinkly skin and stick your nose in their leaves. She says each tree has his own personality, each tree is his very own man. Then you have to make a list of all their beautiful colours.

Not just the greens and the browns, she goes, the greens and browns are the least of it!

She gets all excited when she's talking about trees, her hands stretch up to the sky, her eyes get so shiny sometimes you're afraid she's going to start crying.

Then Olivia Butler stands behind the artist nun, making faces and tapping her finger off the side of her head.

There's a study-hall for doing your ecker and two big recreation halls for after you've finished supper. The white one is for playing games or doing your ballroom dancing. The brown one is for hanging up pictures of your trees, or collecting your letters.

The Headgirl stands on a chair, pulling envelopes out of a sack one by one. She calls out a name then holds the letter up over her head and you can see the bright stamps in the corner for a second, until somebody comes up to snatch it away.

The overseas girls get the best letters: flimsy white envelopes with blue and red stripes all round the edges. Or there's these green ones that have to be unfolded because the letter and the envelope are on the same piece of paper. The Mexican letters have a seal of red wax that has to be broken with a special knife. The Irish letters are usually dead plain.

She never gets any letters.

Flights of stairs around every corner, some wide and long going up five floors. And you could have a right slide for yourself, coming down five floors on the turns and folds of such a long banister. But you'd have to be one of the brave girls and you'd have to be able not to scream your head off. Or else you'd get caught.

There's other stairs too, dark little ones huddled in behind the chapel, and that's where the old nuns sleep. And if you ever sneaked up in the middle of the night and looked through the keyholes a girl called Cassandra said you'd be able to see them asleep, with their gummy mouths wide open and all their baldy heads that look like golfball chewing gums, lying on pillows made out of black stone.

The narrowest stairs go up to the music cells. Then you're in the very, very top of the house and there's a window that you'd just have to step out of and then you'd be dizzy on the roof. Except it's nailed up now on account of the ghost.

The ghost that used to be a Domestic. And she threw herself off the roof because she found out she was getting a baby and she wasn't even married. Jessica McLynn said that's the worst thing you could do, get a baby if you weren't even married. That's a big mortaler. And so is taking your own life. A mortaler means God would have no choice, Jessie said; even if he felt really awful about it, he'd still have to send you straight down to hell.

The music cells would be a very scary place to be sent on a message, walking through the long corridor alone on your tippy-toes. Even when you're at the bottom of the stairs, looking up, listening to the sounds floating down, it's still scary enough. With the plinks and plonks, twings and twangs. Whinges and whines that could be a babyghost.

And a high screeching voice that could be the ghost of its mam.

Mam is getting a new baby. But not for ages yet. And she has a husband so her baby isn't a sin. But every time

Tatty sees the stairs that lead to the music cells and hears all the sounds coming out, she thinks about Mam and her baby, and what if they died, and would they be ghosts then, and where would they go if they were?

When you're in school you think about Dad, telling his funny jokes, making up rhymes. Or going off somewhere in his car, having him all to yourself. Or even sharing him with everyone else sometimes, all squashed together inside.

Like that time at the seaside when it wouldn't stop raining, and the pub wasn't open yet so Mam bought chips for everyone to eat in the car. Then Mam and Dad sang this funny song together, and that was so nice, better than buckets and spades; the car warm with vinegary steam, eating the chips and looking out. At the empty beach and the empty sea. And the rain turning the sand dark brown, and the rain punching holes all over the sea, and the rain popping off the roof of the car, and the rain splodging diamonds all over the windows, and the rain and the rain. And the song that Mam and Dad sang.

She remembers that sometimes at night when she's trying to make herself go to sleep.

In the long dormitory. Where everyone has their own little cubicle. With their own private sink, their own private wardrobe, their own green leather stool and the bed at the wall with the fleecy orange bedspread tucked over a soft sausage pillow.

She loves her little cubicle, the way it's the same as everyone else's, all her things laid out that nobody ever touches so nothing gets broken or lost. And she loves when the shaky nun comes in for inspection, dragging her long finger over the dressing-table, under the bed, on top of the wardrobe, round the rim of the skirting-board. Checking for dust and that she can see her shaky-nun face in the taps. Checking again that you've tucked your sheets in, folded your clothes for the morning – tunic on the bottom, smock for keeping the tunic clean on top, socks and shoes all neat together under the green leather stool. And she loves as well the slow way the shaky nun shows her how to do everything, so she never forgets, and always gets it right, that means she never gets in trouble with her.

She's always paddy-last to go asleep, listening to the sound of the other girls' breathing, trying to guess who owns what snore or who's turning a page of a book under the blankets; whose transistor is that humming under a pillow, fingers dancing its tune across the partition wall.

Then getting up sometimes to look out the windows until her eyes get too tired to see anymore.

January and February: the darkest windows, like a black shiny mirror; the shadow of her face; the stains of wet light from the senior-school block.

March windows are cobwebby-grey before the dark starts leaking through, a little bit later each day. The window till Easter stays daytime bright.

The window in her cubicle looks over the farmyard. You can hear all the animals shuffling and snorting, trying to go off to sleep for the night. You can hear the farm man whistling to himself when he's scraping the brush across the yard like he's scratching a big concrete back. If you open the window you get the milky-weewee smell from the fat white cows. Or the sharp sour stink of pig's poo.

Across in the senior-school block, senior girls fat in their dressing-gowns waddle past windows. Sometimes you can hear their giggly voices; then you might see the floaty grey worms of cigarette smoke creeping out from the common-room window.

But the best window of all is the one out beside the toilets. And you can see over the wall right into the Phoenix Park. You can love the trees the way the artist nun showed you; all their different shapes, their hundreds of colours. But then in the nearly dark they all start looking the same, and there's only one colour.

When it's all dark, there's only their shadows.

Sometimes in the night you might hear someone crying. The most crying happens on Sunday nights or the first night back after holidays. And the most crying comes from the new girls. When a new girl cries in the night then a dorm-nun has to go into her cubicle, tell her to be brave, to say all her prayers.

She was a new girl a few months ago, but no dormnun ever had to go into her.

The girl in the cubicle next door is called Rosemary. She has a blotchy mauve face and her hands and her arms have the same blotchy mauve skin. When she scratches her arm silver skin-flakes fly down on her smock. She says it's because she has a hole in her heart. That makes Tatty wonder if a hole in your heart is the same as a broken heart and if that's why Rosemary cries more than anyone else.

Why are you crying? Tatty whispers to her through the side of the partition.

I'm homesick, she says.

Homesick? What do you mean?

I miss my mummy, she says. I miss her so much.

Tatty tries to think what homesick means and why it makes you cry. When Mam goes mental she might start shouting, I'm sick of this bloody house! I'm sick of it! Sick of it!

But she knows that can't be the same thing.

Then she tries to think what that means, missing your Mummy so much it makes you cry in the night. Except she wouldn't have a Mummy to miss, she'd have a Mam instead.

In her old green school everyone had. Ma, Mammy or Mam. But in her new school nearly everyone has a Mummy or Mum. Except for the foreign girls who have a Mama. And that sounds the best when they say it. Maw-Maw, that sounds so posh.

She closes her eyes and tries to imagine Mam. How nice she looks sometimes, when she's all dressed up and ready to go out, and the way she's such a great singer when she's in good humour. And the time she let Tatty help her make the fat apple cake. And the time she brought Tatty to the night-time pictures, just the two of them together, all on their own on the bus.

She can imagine Mam all right but she's not sure if that means she misses her.

Rosemary cries. Rosemary cries. And it always pushes this question into Tatty's head.

The question is about Mam.

Does Mam ever miss me? the question says.

Does Mam ever miss *me*?

It's the very first Sunday when Dad brings her home and Mam starts giving out through her teeth.

What's she doing here? she goes.

It's Sunday, Dad says.

I know what bloody day of the week it is. What's she doing here? I said.

How do you mean? Dad goes.

How do I mean? How do I mean? I'll tell you how

I mean. It was *your* decision to send her away, now as far as I'm concerned she's either in boarding-school or she's not. She's only been there a week and she's home already. Honest to God you have her ruined. Well let this be the last Sunday. Do you hear me now? I don't want to see her again until mid-term.

But that's six weeks away.

I don't care if it's *sixty* weeks away.

Ah for Jaysus sake, she's ten years old, do you not think now you're being a bit –

She's either in boarding-school or she's NOT, Mam says again.

ᑯ

Six weeks is. Six sevens is. Forty-two days.

The school is a funny place to be on a Sunday. You can walk all around it and hardly meet anyone, you can hear all these noises you wouldn't even notice on any other day of the week. Like the different ticks from different clocks, the water pipes muttering along the walls, the boiler-room having an asthma attack. Or the sounds that come out of the little brown nun when she goes flying up the stairs: flipflop of her habit, soft rosary rattle, sneaky little tinkles from her tuck-shop keys, thinking they're great.

You can hear footsteps coming towards you from two corridors away and then when you meet the footsteps they might turn out to be your own.

If you're a left-over Sunday girl, there's lots of things you can do.

You can go on one of Sister Jarleth's left-over Sunday girls' outings. To the zoo or the museum or maybe just a nature walk out in the Park.

You can go home with a best friend whose mam doesn't mind seeing her on Sunday. You can sit on the warm steps outside the boiler-room and talk to the dark girls. You can stay at the long window at the top of the stairs and watch out for Dad's car in case he sneaks up to see you.

You can do the boiler-room steps and the long window together, if you don't mind your legs being jacked from running up and down stairs all the long day.

When Dad sneaks up to see you, you never know which Sunday it will be because it's a secret from Mam. He says he doesn't even know himself. For example, if she goes to the pub with him on Sunday morning then he won't be able to sneak away, or if she wants him to bring her visiting on Sunday afternoon, or out for a drive-and-a-drink, well then he'll be banjaxed as well.

We'll just have to look on it as a surprise, he says. A surprise for you and a surprise for me.

But how can it be a surprise for the two of us?

Because you won't know which Sunday it'll be. But *I* won't know either.

When Dad does come, he only stays for a minute. He gives you a few bob for yourself even though you tell him there's nowhere to spend it.

He tells you everything you're missing at home and how the new baby is getting along inside Mam's tummy. That size now, he says, showing his fist.

Then he tells you all the other things that are going on behind your back. The new extension that's getting built: a big brand-new kitchen, a bedroom with a door that slides over, two dormer bedrooms made out of the attic, another toilet. And stairs.

Another toilet! *And stairs.*

Then he tells you about Deirdre winning the egg-and-spoon race in her special school.

And that gives her such a pain in her heart thinking about Deirdre crossing over the line, what her face must have been like when she found out she won, her arm held out dead straight and the egg still wobbling in the dip of the spoon.

Except it wasn't an egg, it was a potato, he says, because, God love them, they'd only get broken.

He's holding a big brown paper bag in his arms for her tuck box and she's able to guess where it came from: King crisps and peanuts, small packets of creamcrackers, a couple of Club Milks, a bottle of Club Orange that should need an opener except he must have asked the barman to loosen the cap.

There's four other bottles sticking out of the bag, but Dad says they belong to Mam for when she's watching the

Sunday telly. Each bottle has a gold foil bonnet over its cap that Dad says she can have for her fancy scrapbook collection. She peels them off carefully, only tears one.

Dad pulls the bottles out of the bag and lays them, one by one, on the floor of the car. She wishes she could have the labels as well, because they're so lovely. Blue and gold. Lancer, they say.

CR

Here she's called Carrie. Even by the nuns. Except for this lady teacher who reminds her of Aunt Sal in her mini-skirt and who calls her Cleopatra because of a queen she knows who has the exact same fringe.

And the little brown nun calls her Cara.

Cara is Italian, the little brown nun tells her, digging with a fine comb for nits in her hair. She doesn't know the English for nits, so she calls them little animals instead.

You have bald in your hair Cara, do you know? Yes Sister.

Your mother, does she know?

No Sister, only my brother.

Not your mother?

No Sister.

The little brown nun lifts her hair away from her ear and whispers down into it. You must not be ashamed, Cara. You must not cry. Your mother will take you to the doctor. Then you will grow more beautiful hair. Look how already it grows!

Yes. But then another one always comes.

Your mother will take you to the doctor and no more will come.

When someone calls you Cara it means you're very dear to their heart. *Mia Cara, cara mia.*

She likes being Cara; she likes being Carrie. Better than Caroline, a strict sort of name for when you're in trouble or when you're talking to the aunties which sometimes means the same thing.

But inside her head she's still Tatty.

Here she's a gold-star girl. After only two weeks! That was day number sixteen. That was the best day in school so far. When the teacher-nun said she'd never seen anyone make such progress in all her life, she'd never seen anyone deserve such a gold star. The teacher-nun's name is Sister Dominic. She's in charge of the junior school as well as Tatty's class. And she pinned Tatty's geography project up on the wall and then everyone had to clap.

The first time she got a gold star she wished she could ask for a scissors to cut it out with her name right beside it so she could send it home to show everyone in case they wouldn't believe her. On account of because she's a liar. But after another few days she got so used to seeing it up there on the wall with another one that just grew beside it in the night and another one after that – only silver this time, but still.

And she knew then herself it was really true, that she was a gold-star girl and that they would have to, just *have* to, believe her.

Here she's a best friend. An English girl called Laura Bartok told her that one day, linking her arm, walking back from chapel.

You're my best friend Carrie, Laura said, my *very* best friend.

And that felt a bit funny finding out you were a best friend all of a sudden. That made her want to go off for a while, so she could have a slow think on her own about what being a best friend could mean. A best friend of Laura's. Who the other girls sometimes jeer, taking her off, because they say she's a granny talking like someone out of a book. In fact and indeed. How sweet! And how splendid! I shall and I shan't. One supposes.

She's not a granny, Tatty says. She's not. She's just English, that's all.

And that's how come they're best friends.

So who's yours then? Laura asked her, keeping a tight hold of her arm.

My what?

Best friend?

Mine?

Yes, yours.

Eh well, you can be, if you want, Tatty said, because she felt that was what Laura wanted.

Then Laura asked her to come home with her next Sunday seeing as how they were best friends and all.

She said there'd be roast chicken for dinner. They could eat ice-cream and look at the telly that she called TV. She said they could laugh at her big brother's jokes then play with the toys in her playroom. Then on the way back to school they could stop at the sweet shop and her dad would buy them anything, *anything* they wished, until their tuck boxes were full up to the brim, she said.

Oh and that sounded good. Not just because you'd be out on a Sunday but because you'd have something to think about, all the week before, all the week after. First imagining, then remembering. The face of an English mam, the voice of an English dad. The shape of a playroom.

Or the smell of roast chicken while you're watching the telly, the suck of cold ice-cream off the back of a spoon. The drive back to school then, the taste of a strange car around you, a tuck box on your lap filled up to the brim.

That sounded like the very best way to spend a Sunday.

Yeah! Tatty said. Oh yeah! That'd be – ! Oh yeah thanks for asking, that'd be brillo!

But then at the last minute she had to say no.

On account of Dad and how he might sneak up to see her, and how she might miss him if he did. But she couldn't tell that to Laura, in case he didn't come and then Laura would think she was stupid waiting all day for something that might never be going to happen.

But I've already told my Mum, Laura said. I've told Sister Dominic. I've told everyone, *everyone*. Now why won't you come?

Just don't feel like it, Tatty said.

Well that's that then, Laura said. You can't be my best friend anymore. *In fact* – you can't be my *any* sort of friend, ever again.

These were her Sundays then: the boiler-room steps, the hockey-room when it's raining. Or popping up the stairs now and then to look out for Dad through the long window. But staying with the dark girls for most of the time, the dark girls who never go anywhere and who Dad saw one time and said were like lazy black cats lolling around in the sun. And that she was the tabby cat in the middle.

During the week they all have their own friends, but on Sundays they just have each other.

They always want her to play with them. They always want to mess with her hair, but they can't. Because now the little brown nun fixes it into a plait every day so no one will see her bald patches. Then they ask her to sit down beside them and roll up her sleeve, put her arm into the arm-queue, see all the different colours of skin.

The darkest arm is pitch, pitch black.

The whitest one belongs to Tatty. And it's the only one with freckles. The dark girls love looking at the freckles. They always touch them to see what they feel like. Once one of them reached down and gave her arm a lick, laughing away then for ages with her hands up to her face, white from her teeth, white from her eyes, peeping out from behind shy brown fingers.

The arms in between are nearly black, dark brown, ordinary brown, golden brown, pale brown or there's an American arm that has a different kind of brown and that's called a tan.

Sometimes they give her a spelling test to see if she can guess how to spell the places they come from. Dara Salem; See-eree-a Leonie; Papa New Ginee; U-ganda; New Delly; Mass-ahchew-sus.

She loves the dark girls, the quiet way they play, the way they sing sometimes, soft songs she doesn't understand. The way they ask her to tell them stories about her family and her home, that she sometimes makes up when there's nothing left to tell or when there's something she doesn't want to say out loud. Listening with their eyes, asking loads of questions, listening again. As if it's Tatty that's from some faraway country instead of a house that's just twenty minutes' drive away.

The long window on the fourth-floor landing has the very best view of the school: the gate and the avenue, the grounds outside. So if Dad does come she'll be able to see him from ages away. When she sees his car coming round by the willow tree she nearly bursts herself trying to get down the stairs.

Because she knows if Dad doesn't see her the minute he stops the car then he just drives away. Like he did once before. When she wasn't at the window, and she wasn't on the steps and by the time she spotted his car, it was a few seconds too late, just as it was turning back down the avenue.

She tried to make Dad see her that day, running after his car, screaming, Wait! Wait! She tried to make her legs go harder, her voice louder. She pushed them and she shoved them. Oh please Daddy wait!

But they just wouldn't do what they were told.

Dad's car getting smaller, ducking dark behind the willow tree, smaller and smaller, until in the end it was just a mouthful of something shiny and black, getting swallowed up by the big school gates.

She knew Dad was gone but still couldn't stop screaming, couldn't stop hoping that her voice might be able to catch up with him. To follow him all the way down the avenue, through the gate, along the wall up the country road, into his car even, because he always drives with the window rolled down in case he wants to spit out.

When she turned back around the dark girls were behind her. She couldn't believe they'd gotten up off the steps, to follow her down the avenue, to stand in a silent line behind her.

And it was horrible crying like that for ages in front of them all, seeing them trying to look the other way. Except for a girl called Rosa who just kept giving her these dirty looks up and down.

After a few minutes, Rosa started shouting, Look at you, my God, look! Behaving like a madwoman. Did you never learn to control yourself? And I don't know what you have to cry about anyway – it may be six complete months before *I* see my father again.

For a while she was afraid they might tell the whole school and everyone would think she was a right baby or else a madwoman like Rosa had said.

But she found out later from Laura, after they became best friends again, that the dark girls never tell on anyone, *in fact*, the dark girls never tell.

When the bell goes for tea, that's the best part of Sunday. Then she can leave the long window alone. Because it's too late now and she knows Dad won't be coming. And that's a funny way to feel when that happens, not even sad, not disappointed. That's a feeling that's free and glad.

Nothing to do only take her time coming back down the stairs. Go into the refectory, sit at her table. Empty Sunday chairs all around her. Iced buns, triangles of cheese, a whole sliced pan and butter all to herself for tea.

CR

Mam brings her to see this doctor called a Specialist during the first mid-term break. Dad leaves the money for a taxi on the table and a cheque to pay the doctor for looking at Tatty's head. The cheque doesn't say Doctor. The cheque says Mr P-r-something.

That's because you don't call him Doctor, Mam explains in the taxi to Tatty and Jeannie. He's higher up than a doctor. That's why you call him Mister. And that's why you don't call his office a surgery, you call it his rooms.

Jeannie isn't listening to Mam; she just stays looking out the taxi window all the way into town. And the taximan doesn't say anything either, listening to his radio, joining in the songs. So it's just her and Mam.

Mam starts laughing at the taximan's singing, giving her a little nudge. So Tatty starts laughing as well, even though she doesn't really know why it's funny. She feels like she's Mam's pal that day, the two of them laughing behind the taximan's back. She even feels that Mam might like her.

A few days ago, she didn't feel that, when she first got home after six weeks away. Then Mam didn't even look pleased to see her. She said, My God, you're gone some size, you're as *fat*. What the hell are they feeding you up in that place anyway? You'd think it was you that was expecting and not me.

Then Mam went out with Aunt Sal.

The Doctor's rooms turns out to be only one room. In a house that looks like the house in *Mary Poppins*. With steps up to the front door and a hall inside with leather armchairs at the side and a vase with tall flowers and a typing lady who says, If you'd like to take a seat, to Jeannie, and, If you'd like to just step this way, to her and Mam.

Mam looks very nice sitting on the edge of a sofa talking to the doctor while he fills out a form. She's wearing her new dress called a maternity smock and her good coat and her good voice for when she's talking to strangers.

There's a pair of long windows behind her and you can see outside: the railings of the house and the curly trees in the park across the road and the busy people passing by that she wishes would look in so she can see what kind of faces they have, but who never do.

The doctor has a funny smell off him, a smell of nearly perfume.

He looks at the holes in Tatty's hair. He says they're called alo-somethings.

His waistcoat is stripy and there's little gold medals in the cuff of his sleeves. He keeps pulling strands of her hair up by his fingertips. Any strands that come away he flicks into the air, and then she's scared in case he's going to make another alo-something. Like the one in his own head, much bigger than any of her ones, spreading from the top nearly all the way down to his ears.

His belly is a bit fat in his stripy waistcoat; his shoes have pointy toes.

Any other health problems? he asks.

I don't know Mister, Tatty answers.

I was talking to your mother, he says then, and that makes her face go red.

He tells her to wait outside.

Jeannie is out in the hall, thinking she's great on the big leather armchair, reading a big woman's magazine, flipping her thumb off her tongue before she turns a page over.

What did he say? she asks.

Nothing.

He did so, I heard him.

Well what are you asking me for then?

The typing woman has a brown bun in her hair. Her typewriter is much bigger than Mam's one and makes a different sound, softer and slower like a purr. She looks up for a second, gives Tatty a smile. She has two long wires sticking out of her ears. When the telephone rings she pulls one of the wires out of one of her ears, puts it back in then as soon as she's finished speaking.

Jeannie puts the magazine back in the pile and moves right up to the door of the doctor's room. She calls Tatty over with her hand.

We can't do that Jeannie. We can't go on an earwig, not *here*.

Shhhh, Jeannie goes. She's saying something about you.

What? What?

She's saying you're very highly strung.

What does that mean?

Don't know.

Now he's asking her if everything is all right at home.

And what's she saying?

Shhhh. He's asking if she gets on with her husband. And what?

Jeannie turns away from the door for a minute.

Fucken liar! she says in a whisper that sounds very loud. JEANNIE!

Well she is.

You shouldn't be cursing, Tatty says, looking over at the typing lady. You're always cursing these days. I'm straight telling if you ever do it again. Do you hear me? I am.

The typing lady looks up again, smiles and looks down.

Jeannie puts her ear back up to the door.

If Mam finds out about all the cursing you've been doing you'll be in for it. You'll be –

Ah fuck her, is all Jeannie says.

JEANNIE!

Here, I know what they're called, Jeannie says. What?

Them yokes in your hair.

So do I.

What then?

They're alo-somethings.

Alo-peeshas, Jeannie corrects her. And guess what?

What?

He says there's no cure for them.

By the time mid-term break is over, Mam doesn't like her again.

She even sends her back to school a day too early by mistake. Even though Tatty keeps telling her, I don't think it's till tomorrow, Mam. I'm sure it's not till tomorrow.

You needn't start any of your tricks, Mam goes. You needn't think I don't know what you're at – trying to dodge going back to school.

I'm not Mam. I swear, I'm sure it's tomorrow.

I knew this would start. I just bloodywell knew it! Trying to dodge going back. Well a pity about you is what I say – you've made your bed now you better get ready to lie in it.

She tries to tell Dad when she gets in the car and again when they get to the school. But Dad says they're a bit early that's all, that's why there's no other cars and anyway Mam would never, *ever*, make such a stupid mistake.

Walking around in the empty school, counting the steps on the stairs. Looking through glass panels on doors that are locked. Peeping through keyholes into silent rooms.

Then the dark started coming. First it just sneaked in slow. Then it got thicker inside. Faster and faster, she could see it doing tumbles in front of her up the long corridors, filling up corners, blocking off stairs.

All dark then, and still no one else in the school. She tried to turn on a light. Then she tried to turn on another one. But the electricity must have been switched off. That's when she really started to get afraid.

The telephone box on the wall. Blind fingers patting around for the penny slot, the holes on the dial, the slide down to press button A.

Mam! she said. Mam, oh thank God. There's nobody here, it's dark and I'm on my own. It's the wrong day. I told you it was. It's tomorrow. I told you! I told you, I did!

But Mam said if it was a mistake there was nothing she could do about it now, that Tatty would just have to make the best of it, that's all.

What?

Well there's not much I can do about it from here, is there?

But Mam everywhere's locked, the door to the senior school, the classrooms, the dorms. I've nowhere to sleep even.

It's only one day and I don't know where your father is, Jesus! There must be someone around.

No Mam there isn't.

Look. I'm up to my eyes here: Deirdre's acting up and Luke's not well. I've a bloody pain in my back, can hardly walk. Now I'm sorry but.

Mam please.

What do you want me to do? Put Luke in the pram and drag the lot of us over there? Get over to the convent, you'll find one of the nuns.

I'd have to go outside to get to the convent and it's dark. It's dark.

Well what about the senior school then?

I told you I can't the door is –

Beep beep beep beep.

Then Mam was gone.

No pennies left.

She had to make herself stop crying, shoving her hand over her mouth to squash back the sobs because she couldn't bear the sound of them hopping around on their own in the dark. She picked up the phone, put it back down, up, down a few more times, trying to think what to do, trying to not look out the window at the Park outside. She hated the trees then, the big monster trees, with their wrinkly bodies and their long sharp claws and mad hair shaking when they whispered together about how they were going to get at her across the big wall if she even put one foot outside to get to the convent. She picked up the phone again and rang the operator. Then she was talking to someone in Myo's.

Ten minutes later, Dad was there.

Twenty minutes later she was home.

Mam starts laughing when she sees her coming in, standing there like Humpty-Dumpty with her hand pushed into her back.

Well I might have known, she says, I might have known you'd get around your father, you little scallywag.

Then she asks her if she wants a bit of dinner. I'm not hungry, Tatty says.

But you're always hungry.

I'm not. I'm going to bed.

Come here, what's wrong with you?

I know now you don't want me, she said to Mam. *What?* What in the name of God are you talking about?

I know now. I know NOW.

❧

When you're at home, you think about school, the way there's always loads of people to play with and everyone says her Carrie name, linking her arm, walking along.

And the sunlight sliding over the classroom when the teacher-nun is reading out a story that's making her laugh so much you can't really hear what she's saying. With the laughing tears running down her face, hand squeezing down on the laughing pain in her stomach. So in the end the teacher-nun has to ask for a volunteer to finish the story off.

Then all arms jump up: SISTER! SISTER! Me, sistersister.

Except for Tatty, because when Tatty puts up her hand, MAMMY! MAMMY! bursts out of her mouth instead.

She nearly died then with the whole class laughing behind her.

But the teacher-nun gave her this lovely smile that showed she didn't mind. And then she loved the teacher-nun so much she wished she could hug her. Then she loved the teacher-nun so much she wished she could be her really Mam.

1973

SHE GETS A LETTER! NEARLY FAINTS WHEN SHE hears her name being called out, sees the envelope high in the Headgirl's hand. And all the faces that turn to look at her: from the crowd still standing around the Headgirl, to those at the wall already reading letters. Because it's such a strange thing to happen. Her getting a letter, the first one ever, after nearly two years in school.

The Headgirl calls her name out again.

Everything about the envelope in her hand gives her a thrill then: its thick lavender paper, her own name there, that gorgeous handwriting, fountain-pen ink – not even a smudge.

Her letter makes everyone nosy, a little group tightening around her, and that gives her a thrill as well.

Who's it from Carrie?

Don't know.

Open it then. Go on. Open it.

There's designs on the inside of the flap when she eases it open and a smell that pops out like talcum powder. She holds the envelope up and one by one the noses come down to take a sniff. She sees the fold of the pages inside, lavender again – *matching*.

She takes out the letter, looks at the bottom of the last page for a signature.

Oh.

What?

It's from my sister. My big sister Jeannie. She's two years older then me, fourteen, in secondary school.

She doesn't notice the photograph slipping from the pages and falling on the floor because she's so surprised at Jeannie sending her a letter, and the strangeness of Jeannie's handwriting too, large and clear, because usually when you see her writing it's on one of those mad little notes, tight tiny stitches you can barely read.

Laura picks up the photo and hands it to her.

Oh look, it's my baby brother. He's started to walk. I can't wait to see him. It seems like such ages. Only ten more days.

The photo is handed around and a big *ahhhhh* comes out on a long single note.

Tatty is bursting with pride.

Olivia wants her to read the letter out loud, but Laura tells her to mind her own business. Letters are private, Laura says, and Carrie may prefer to read it alone – try the classroom Carrie, the bell doesn't ring for another ten minutes.

She smiles her best friend smile at Laura.

She goes into the classroom, sits on the window sill, feels the winter sun warm on her back through the glass. Then she props the photo of Michael against a window pane, watches him turn pale with light. She opens the pages again.

The letter is perfect, like everything Jeannie does. Address in the corner, date underneath. Yours sincerely down at the bottom.

P.S. When are you coming home?

She takes another sniff of the paper and then starts to read.

Her hands are shaking when she's finished the letter. She waits for a minute till they settle down, then goes to her desk, takes out her fancy scrapbook collection, opens it out. In the seam between pages she slots the empty envelope, then squeezes the photo of Michael behind it.

The bell screams through the corridors, making her jump. She stuffs Jeannie's letter up her sleeve, goes out to the toilet and locks herself in. Sits down then and reads it again.

Dear Tatty,

I'm off sick so I'm writing. Do you like this paper? I fecked it out of Copeland's, nice isn't it? Doctor came, needle in the bare bum for me. More tablets for Mam for her stupid depression. Do you know what? She hasn't stopped bawling in weeks even worse than when after Michael was born or else she's pissed all the time. God I'm sick of her. You'll see for yourself when you get home if you still don't believe me. Felt like spilling the beans to the Doctor about what's going on here but don't worry I didn't. You don't know because you're NEVER here but things have been really crap for the last few weeks. Worse row ever two weeks ago. Wait till you hear this. You know the way she used get in the end of one of our beds when they had a row. Yak! Don't remind me.

Well she doesn't do that anymore. Because now she's moved upstairs into the extension, *my* room if you don't mind. Yours as well when you bother your arse coming home. So I don't know where you're supposed to sleep now. I was in with Deirdre for a while but couldn't bear the noises of Mam next door so now I sleep on the sofa (don't tell or I'll burst you). Anyway she's made a stupid flat for herself up there. Mental she is, off her bloody rocker. MY room. To top it all doesn't Deirdre get her you-know-whats a couple of weeks ago, had a complete sevener. I was left to deal with it all. She kept running out of the jacks waving the s.t. all over the place or else trying to put a plaster on herself because she thought it was a cut. Tell you about it when you get home. I have to do everything now on my own. The house is in a right mess. Dad took her housekeeping off her and put me in charge instead. He even gave me his OWN watch for keeps for doing such a good job. Jealous? Ha ha, bet you are. So she hates me now. I don't care I hate her too, Dad as well. You as well for leaving me here, while you're off having a great time in your poxy posh school. With your poxy posh friends Laura that you went to stay with at midterm instead of coming home and moustache-face Olivia and that other one, fat one with the boy haircut and the stupid name, Cassandra or whatever you call her.

Yours sincerely,

Jeannie.

P.S. When are you coming home?

She crumples the pages up, rubs them between the flat of her hands, again and again. A heap of paper crumbs on her lap. She stands up, flaps her skirt out over the toilet bowl. A swirl of lavender tossing on water, flushing away.

Laura's eyes nearly pop out while she's telling her about Jeannie's letter. She's a hold of Tatty's arm in the back of the hockey-room, and the more Tatty tells her the harder she squeezes.

Laura says Jeannie must be *absolutely* mad, making up such shocking lies.

Such a bitch, Laura says. Such a horrible *bitch*. I'm glad I don't have sisters, if that's the way they go on. And to say those mean things about all your friends. You know what's the matter with her?

What?

She's jealous of you.

Of me?

Yes. She's trying to spoil things for you. And jealous because you came to my house for mid-term and we had such fun. We did have a great time. Didn't we?

Oh yeah.

Do you know what I'd do, if I was you?

What?

I'd tell my Dad.

I couldn't.

You ought. Serve her right. Or your Mum even. Imagine if she knew Jeannie was saying such things! Mmm. Imagine.

Don't tell me you believe her Carrie?

Oh no.

Horrible lies. Horrible bitch.

Yes, Tatty says, she was always a liar. I wouldn't believe one word she says.

I don't. I won't.

I'd just put that letter straight out of my head.

Tatty squeezes her eyes, and it's gone.

ભ

It comes back again, two weeks later on the first day of the Christmas holidays when she sees Dad sitting in the car outside the school.

Dad's drunk. His eyes are too soft, hands too stiff on the steering-wheel. He's rocking on his seat, pushing his face over the steering-wheel up to the window then pulling it back again, one eye half-open. Like he's practising how he's going to see the road once the car starts moving again.

She knows he's drunk the minute she sees him, but he keeps on telling her anyway.

In case you don't know, he says, I'm Mickey Monk.

Who?

Drunk.

Then he holds out his hand and tells her to give him a smack for being so bold.

There's a Christmas tree hanging out the boot of the car and it looks like a big fox's tail in the dark. There's all these hams squashed on the front seat and a couple of turkeys in a box on the floor. There's another turkey all on his own, droopy neck flopped out on the back seat, a dripping of blood hanging out of his beak.

She has to sit beside the turkey. There's no room for her suitcase either. So Dad gets out and spends ages trying to get it to fit into the boot with the tree. Ages and ages. And that's another way to know he's drunk because he's never that slow.

He's like *that*! is what Mam says, clicking her fingers when she's talking about how quick Dad is. Like *that*!

And she thinks now it's a good job Dad was miles late coming to collect her for the Christmas holidays. Because at least there's no one left to see the state of him bashing the suitcase around, grunting and cursing, or trying to be funny saying stupid things like the tree keeps biting his hand.

A while ago she didn't think it was such a good job, him being so late, a while ago she was raging, fed up with hanging around for hours, sitting on her suitcase looking out the long window. Hours of saying Happy Christmas, over and over, the amount of times getting fewer and fewer till it was only now and then, till it was never again. Because there was nobody left to say it to. Except for the sewing-nun who's a bit simple, coming in every few minutes, going – Daddy not here yet? Still not here yet? Then trying to get her to go to tea in the nun's ref and telling her all about the special mass they were having on Christmas Day, the beautiful singing, the cakes then for after, the big chimneys that a certain Mister Santa Claus can slip down without any bother.

As if she was going to have to spend Christmas in school. As if Dad wasn't coming at all.

Dad's drunk. He tells her again and again while he's driving along dead slow, rocking on his seat and looking like someone out of Deirdre's special school.

I know Dad, you told me about twenty times already. You're drunk.

And that's how come they crash the car. Even though he said it was because of the ice on the hill and the watery lights on that part of the road and that stupid bastard

Jackie Mac who was supposed to have got the new tyres on. Not to mention the thick who came up with the idea of putting the pole there in the first place.

Crashing the car makes him stop being drunk for a while. Turning around to see if she's all right in the back seat, patting her face, her head, her arms, to make sure everything is still where it was before he crunched into the pole.

I'm *all right*, I said, Dad. *Leave* me.

Making her move her legs and her feet anyway and then going on about the hams. Thank God for the hams, thank God for the hams. Thank God for the hams.

When he jumps out of the car, he's back to his old quick self.

He tells her she has to get out as well, but she wants to look for her bar of Morny soap that hopped out of her hands with the jerk of the car.

The Morny soap that she won for coming third in the class and that she'd been holding up to her nose and over her mouth since they left the school. To block the smell of the car like a butcher's shop and the smell of the car like a pub.

She just wanted the feel of it again in her hand, the soft smell through its fancy paper, the invisible taste.

I'm not leaving without my soap, she shouts at Dad, even though she knows he doesn't care because it was only for coming third in the class.

Third? he'd said when she told him. Third, is that all? Jeannie always comes first.

But it was dead hard getting third, Dad. There's loads of really brainy girls in my class. Some of them even can speak three languages.

Ah third is no use, no use. Oul third. Come back to me when you're first.

And that's when they crashed the car.

When Dad jumps out of the car this woman sticks her head out a cottage window on the side of the road and asks them if they're all right.

There's no one hurt, Dad shouts out to her. No one hurt, that's all that matters.

I can't even come out to you, the woman goes, me leg's in a plaster.

There's no one hurt.

What about the young one?

I'd a load of hams in the front so the young one was in the back – thank God for the hams.

Hams?

Christmas boxes for the customers and that.

Oh? And me husband isn't even here.

That's all right mam, thanks all the same, we'll manage, he goes, shoving his arm in through the window to steer the car straight, into a shadow on the side of the road, away from the pole.

And I'm not even on the phone. Two doors down's on the phone though, you could try there.

No need to concern yourself, thanks just the same, I'll phone in the village.

What about your hams?

I'll be back for them.

He locks up the car, then opens it again, pulls out a ham, dusts it off, straightening its skin like it's material on a skirt.

You wait here, he says to Tatty.

She can hear him talking low to the woman, sees him then stuffing the ham in her window.

He comes back to the car. That should help to keep her mouth shut, he says. I'd say they haven't a pot to piss in.

He starts getting a bit drunk again, walking down the road to get to Chapelizod village, not falling but not walking straight either, just doing these little curtseys after every few steps, bumping off her arm, driving her mad.

You're shivering, he says. Are you cold? Do you want my coat?

No.

Are you sure?

That's stupid Dad, your coat'd be swimming on me.

Oh right. Are you upset?

No.

I suppose you'll tell.

No.

Are you hungry? I'll get you something nice in the chipper when we get home. How about a nice long juicy ray?

No.

No? No? No? Is that the only word the nuns teach you up in that fancy school?

He bursts into the pub and starts making a right show of them, roaring and shouting all over the place about how there's been a bit of an accident and how he's feeling a bit shook and wants a double brandy now, now, now, this minute.

When the barman gives him the glass of brandy, he holds it up and slowly turns it around in the air, like he wants to make sure everyone in the pub can see it. It reminds her of the priest in mass the way he does that.

For the shock, he goes, the shock.

The brandy flops back into his mouth. He scrunches his face up, snarls like a dog, shaking his head. He wallops the glass down on the counter. Same again. And again.

She goes into the toilet and sees a smear of blood on her face. She touches the blood and tastes it off the tip of her finger. When she washes her face, the blood is all gone, no sign of even a tiny cut or a scratch that it might have come out of. Then she looks down at her bar of Morny soap and sees there's blood on its fancy paper.

It takes her a minute to know the blood doesn't belong her, it belongs to the turkey. And it's in her mouth. She sticks out her tongue, holds it under the running tap, making the kind of noises you do when you're getting sick. *Ghaaaaagh.*

When she comes back outside Dad is drunk again. Drunker even than he was the first time around. We'll go home now, he says. Those oul brandies have gone straight to me head. I wouldn't mind, he tells the barman, but I hadn't a drop all day. But I must have had – what? – four doubles there, I was that shook. Don't forget that now, if anyone comes calling.

Like anyone in particular? the barman asks.

I think you know who I mean.

Dad puts a pound note under the empty glass of brandy and slides it to the barman across the counter. The barman slides the glass off the counter, gives a bit of a nod, then turns away.

This man Dad knows and his skinny-malink wife drive them home.

Dad sits in the back beside Tatty. And that's the first time she remembers ever sitting in the back of a car with Dad, and the first time she's ever seen Dad in a car that he wasn't driving, and the first time as well that it feels like he isn't in charge.

The man and woman are a bit drunk too, but not as much as really drunk Dad. He gets the first prize. The woman comes second. The man only comes oul third.

The woman has these letting-on eyebrows nearly up to her hair and that makes her a bit mad looking. There's black scratches on her sticky-out teeth and she's sitting sideways with her back to the door so she can smoke her cigarette in at Dad. She's either laughing at nothing or else asking these really stupid questions. When you answer one of her stupid questions she gets a big shock. Then goes on like she doesn't believe you.

Ah would you look at herself in there, the woman says, in her blue uni-form. Aren't you only gorgeous in there in your blue uni-form, sitting in there beside your Da, God love you. How old are you now?

I'm nearly twelve.

Nearly twelve? Ah you couldn't be. Are you the youngest?

No. I'm in the middle.

In the middle? Are you sure?

Well … I'm not *dead* in the middle since Michael was born because now I have two big sisters and three little brothers. But I used to be in the middle.

But you're not now?

No.

See? I knew you were having me on. What class are you in anyway?

Sixth.

Sixth? Ah go away out of that. Do you still believe in Santy?

No.

NO? You do so, you big liar.

Then Dad starts getting really stupid as well, talking with this whine in his voice, the words sliding round in his mouth.

Do you see this little girl here, he says, bouncing his palm off the top of Tatty's head. She's the best little girl in the world. Not a word of a lie. I tell you somethin' now – will I? Will I tell you somethin' now? If you were to travel, say, to every country, I mean *every*. In the whole wide … You wouldn't find better. Do you know now what she is? Will I tell you now what she is – she's her Daddy's pal, that's what she is. His best oul pal. Her Daddy's best.

Your best pal? Ah you're jokin' me?

And she's on her Christmas holliers, I hope you know.

Already? That couldn't be right. My lot's not off till next week.

She's in boarding-school, they get longer holidays.

Bore-din' school? I don't believe you. *Bore-din' school?* Oh well excuse me.

They stop at Dad's car. I'd give you a hand, he says to the man, passing him the keys. I'd give you a hand only …

I know, says the man, you're bollixed.

Exactly.

It takes the man a good while to empty Dad's car, getting in and out of the cold every few minutes. Because every time he thinks he's finished Dad keeps remembering something else.

After the hams in the front and the turkeys in the box, there's all the papers in the cubby hole. After the papers in the cubby hole, there's the envelopes under the driver's seat. After the envelopes under the driver's seat there's Tatty's suitcase in the boot.

In, out. In, out; puffing clouds of white cold from Dad's car to his.

I'll have to leave the tree, he says to Dad, sitting back into the car, turning the key, blowing into his fists, then putting them around the steering-wheel like he thinks he's all finished at last.

Ah don't worry about it, Dad says. Leave the fucken thing.

Leave the fucken thing? the woman screams out. Do you hear him? *Leave the fucken thing?* What about the poor kids? What about their little Christmas?

Ah I'll get it again or I'll get them another one. Anyway it's too bloody early for a tree. Christmas is not for – what? Another week anyway. Too early. Am I right or am I wrong?

I don't know what you are, the woman says.

The man starts driving away.

Hold it, Dad goes. Hold it. Hold it.

Wha'?

The turkey in the back seat.

The wha'?

There was another turkey in the back – it must have fallen on the floor. For the bank manager. Whatever you do, don't forget that.

Ah here, the man goes. What do you think I am?

When the man gets the turkey he doesn't take it around to the boot of his car. He goes to the passenger door this time and taps on the window.

Ah what do you want? the woman says, like she's annoyed because now she'll have to turn around and won't be able to look at Dad every minute. Ah wha'?

Open the window there for a second, the man says. Go on, open it, quick.

She rolls down the window. The turkey's face hops up, dives in at her, snuffling all over her hair.

Paaah, chuck chuck chuck, the man goes, holding the turkey up by the neck. *Paaah chuck chuck*.

Get away from me, the woman starts screaming. Her hands go up to her face, head ducks down to her knees. Get away, I said. *Awaaaay*.

Then the man can't stop laughing, leaning over the bonnet, trying to catch his breath. He brings the turkey up over the bonnet, pecking his beak off the front window.

Howiye, the turkey says in through the window. Howiye, any chance of an oul gobble in there?

Then the woman goes mental. You mad bastard, she screams at him. You mad fucken alky.

The man stops laughing then. He goes round to the back of the car to put the turkey in the boot.

Mad alcoholic, she says again. In getting dried out twice last year and look at him, mouldy again. They must have dryin' out his brain while they were at it.

Dad tips Tatty on the leg. He nods his head at the front of the car then rolls up his eyes. Pay no attention, he whispers. Lunatics, the pair of them.

He tips her again. It wasn't a real crash, he says. It was only a little bump.

Yes Dad.

Then he starts whining again, You know your old Dad wouldn't do anything to hurt you, don't you?

Yes Dad, I do.

When the woman turns back around her letting-on eyebrows are smudged all over her forehead. And then she's *really* mad looking. Tatty feels a big laugh coming up through her throat ready to burst out, but when she looks at the woman a bit longer the laugh slides back down.

The man slams the door getting back into the car.

See you, the woman says pointing her finger in his face, see you. You're only a bollix. Disgustin' you are.

Ah shut up, will you? It was a joke. A JOKE.

Disgustin' – isn't he? she asks Tatty.

I don't know, Tatty says.

They move off and it's for good this time, back down through the village, past the pub where Dad drank all his double brandies. She can see the barman at the window fixing a crib; holy Jesus with the animals around him, his mam and dad smiling down. There's a cardboard cut-out of Santa on the other window, one side of his face squeezed into a wink, a sack over his shoulders, bottles of drink poking out. Behind the Santa through the top corner of the window, the pubtelly high on a wall, little people running around, a big face talking, little people again.

They turn into the dark shortcut, where they sometimes play knick-knack on the way back to school. Cottages squashed in tight together, a man standing on the corner who gives them a wave, out again onto the main road, bright sudden light stinging her eyes.

Dad's head is wandering around on the back of the seat; his eyes are trying to stay open but you can tell he's asleep by his breathing. The woman doesn't mind if he's asleep but – she keeps staring at him anyway, lighting one cigarette off another.

Look at him, she says to Tatty. He's Langer-oo. Oh God, wait'n your Ma sees him. Then the woman starts grinning like mad as if that's going to be funny

Until Dad wakes up shouting.

And calls Mam a cunt.

He doesn't say who he's talking about, but Tatty knows who he means. She also knows it must be the worst curse in the world by the way it makes the skinny woman stop grinning, by the way it makes her eyes stare hard, even though she didn't seem to mind all the curses in the car up to now, hearing them and even saying most of them herself. But she minds now all right.

She's only a cunt, Dad says again. I wouldn't be in this state only for that dirty rotten cunt.

The woman's eyes close down to a slit. She holds a curl of smoke in her mouth for a second then quickly twists herself back around to the front.

Dad falls asleep again.

Ah don't mind him, the man in the front says to the skinny woman, he's plastered.

There's no call for it, the woman says.

The man pats his wife on the leg, It's only a word, he says. Only a word.

They go up a black hill and the rain comes at them, frosty and soft, melting like ice-cream all over the window. Tatty closes her eyes, pretending to be asleep. She listens to the ticking of windscreen wipers.

CR

Home. And the house is all dark like there's nobody in or else they've all gone to bed. That seems a bit odd because, even though it's late, it'd be still early enough for Mam and Jeannie to be up watching the telly, the telly she's been dying for all week.

Dad's still asleep. She goes to wake him but the man says she might as well leave him be till the stuff's out of the car and in the hall. Then he opens the front door with Dad's keys.

Here we go again, he says going round to the boot, and because she feels sorry for the man then, and because she doesn't want to stay with his skinny-malink wife as well, she gets out to give him a hand.

But first she waits till he already has the turkey safe in the hall, in case he expects her to carry it, or in case he starts *pah-chuckchuck*ing again

The man can't wake Dad all the way, so he has to carry him half-asleep like a big puppet into the house. With Dad's head hanging down to his chest as if his neck's broken, and his arm shooting out now and then to steady himself off a wall. Even when there is no wall, his arm still does that.

He doesn't sleep upstairs, Tatty tells the man when he gets Dad into the hall. My Mam and Dad's room is down there, through the living-room, second door on the left.

Thank Christ for that in anyway, says the man.

Will I get my Mam first?

Your Mam? Oh right your Mam. Ah no don't bother.

Tatty stays in the hall while the man puts Dad to bed. Then looks up the stairs to the room at the top, starts thinking about Jeannie's letter again. The door opens sharply, and there's Mam. She can only see three-quarters of Mam: her slippers, her dressing-gown up to her sleeves. But not her face. She opens her mouth to call up to Mam.

But the door at the top of the stairs slams shut before she has a chance to say anything.

When the man comes back out to the hall he leans down to Tatty, saying she's a very good girl. Then he tells her Dad's not a bad man.

I know that, Tatty says.

Of course you do. It's just that things aren't the best at the minute, so, you know, don't blame him if …

If what?

Ah nothin'.

Then he says he has something for her.

First he gives her Dad's keys to mind; then he gives her a whole pound all to herself. She tries not to take the pound but the man keeps going, Take it outa that, go on, take it. It's your Christmas box. A Christmas box. From me to you.

Then he stuffs the note into her pocket.

The streetlights come in through the porch and it's the first time she gets a good look at his face. Even though she already knows the shape of him so well, and the sound of his voice from the ages they've spent together in the very same car, it feels like she's only just met him. She thinks for a minute she might tell him about her prize for coming third in the class. But in the end she just says, Oh thanks very much for the pound.

She stands at the front door and waves at the man going backwards down the drive in his car. The man waves back. When he gets to the gate he rolls down his window, sticks out his head.

Happy Christmas Caroline!

Happy Christmas.

His skinny-malink wife doesn't budge.

She's not sure what to do then, with the house so silent and dark.

Her stomach is rumbling, her throat feels that dry, the kitchen is only a few steps away, the telly only next door in the living-room. Mam's just up the stairs. But.

She takes off her shoes, sits on her suitcase and waits.

A whisper flies out from the back of the hall, *TATTY!*

She turns around and there's Jeannie's shadow.

Jeannie! You're after giving me such a –

Shush. Keep your voice down. Come here, come on.

She follows Jeannie into the alcove under the new stairs in the room that used to be the old kitchen but is supposed to be part of a new bigger hall now, even though there's still bits of the old kitchen there: a press on the wall with the door hanging off, a lump of metal poking out where the taps of the sink used to be, the old washing-machine blocking the alcove that Jeannie has just squeezed behind.

Who's your man? Jeannie asks, moving up on her cushion so Tatty can sit down beside her.

Tatty ducks in. He gave us a lift home. Oh Jeannie, wait till you hear about Dad –

Shhhh.

Where's everybody?

In bed.

I saw Mam upstairs. Is she really – ?

Mam? Oh wait till *you* hear about Mam.

So Jeannie starts telling her all about Mam in her makey-up flat. And it's like she's talking about someone out of a book or out of a film she's seen on the telly. As if it's nothing got to do with them, as if it's just a good story to tell in the dark.

Mam's taken the record-player up to her flat and the red transistor radio that she leaves on the whole night long. She even has a Primus stove for making her dinner and she's turned one of the built-in wardrobes into a press like as if it's a kitchen: tins and packets on the top shelf where there used to be jumpers. Cup, plate, bowl, a few scraps of cutlery on the bottom shelf where there used to be shoes.

She keeps a beaker and plastic plate for Michael there too, because he's the only one she ever lets in the room.

Michael doesn't like staying in Mam's flat for too long, even though he bangs the door himself to get in because he keeps forgetting that, once he gets in, it won't be that easy get out again. When Mam lets him in she wants him to stay, but he hates being locked in. You can hear him toddling around for a while; then he starts banging on the door to get out. After a while he starts screaming crying until Mam opens the door again and throws him out on the landing.

Throws him?

Well …

Throws him?

Sort of just shoves him.

When you go into her room you have to knock first. But you wouldn't really bother unless she was wanted on the phone or something like that. Sometimes she doesn't answer, sometimes she does.

When you go into her flat there's this funny smell of lead. Like the smell of a pencil case, only bigger. Jeannie says that's the smell of vodka.

Jeannie knows this because one time when Mam went out she got in the window and found all these bottles under the bed. Empty, they were. Two big ones, three medium ones and a whole lot of little baby ones as well.

She got in the window because the lock on the door is like the lock you'd see on a front door. If you wanted to open it from the outside, you'd have to have a halldoor key. Or else you'd have to put your foot right through it. Like Dad did one night, Jeannie says.

He broke down the door?

Yes. Then Mam called the police.

The police? The police were here?

The police. Oh God, don't start crying. You weren't even here.

I know but –

You *don't* know. You weren't even here. You haven't even been here since September.

I know, I'm sorry. It was Laura's birthday and she asked me for mid-term and, and I –

It doesn't matter now.

Mam wanted the police to arrest Dad, Jeannie said, but they wouldn't. They said there was a pair of them in it and they should be ashamed of themselves in front of their own children. Then the police went away. When Mam called the police, she was drunk. But when the police came she was sober. Jeannie says that's because she probably went into the jacks upstairs and made herself puke, sticking her fingers right down her throat.

Dad was still a bit drunk so the police gave out to him more.

After they went away Dad sat on the sofa for ages, with his hands up to his face. Then he got up and just went into bed. You could hear Mam dragging the chest of drawers over to the door so no one could open it. Then the next day she got the lock fixed again.

Oh God, poor Dad.

Poor Dad? Don't make me laugh. They're as bad as each other, even the policeman knew that. Anyway you always stick up for him because you're his pet.

Well? You're Mam's one.

No I'm not, I just pretend to be to keep out of trouble. Because I'm not stupid like you and Brian. But you? You're *really* his pet, always going off everywhere with him, leaving me here on my own, even though I'm two years older than you. Ever since we were small, you've been doing that.

You were sick all the time. You could have been his pet too, only for that.

Jeannie takes her inhaler out of her pocket, gives it a rattle, bites down and sucks in. She holds onto her breath for a few seconds; when she lets it out again the words are tight and high. Well I wouldn't be his pet *now*, not if you paid me, she says.

Then she continues with her story about Mam.

Before Mam moved into the extension she ran away for two weeks. And then Dad took Jeannie out of school to be in charge of the house. When Mam came back she told Jeannie to move her stuff out of the room; that's when she turned it into a flat. Nobody knows where Mam went, not Alice, not Sal, not even the aunties. Dad phoned them all up, then called to their houses, then phoned them again. Nobody knew. Nobody still knows. Only Mam.

But the aunties must know what's going on now?

Bits. She tells them what she wants them to know. Like Dad putting his foot through the door maybe, and the rows, she tells them about the rows, but only what he says, never what she says herself.

Well why don't you tell them then?

Hah! As if they'd listen. Anyway you couldn't tell them about the rows now.

Why not?

The rows are different now. How?

They just are.

When Mam wants a cup of tea she fills up a pot out of the sink in the upstairs jacks then heats it up on her Primus stove. She hardly ever goes into the new kitchen either, except maybe to take something out of the fridge. She doesn't even make the dinner anymore. Not since Dad stopped giving her money, because he says she'll only spend it on drink.

Oh Jeannie, that's awful!

No it's not. Look.

Jeannie takes a big torch out from behind her back, switches it on. A skin of lacy light spreads over the alcove. Then she pulls this big wellington boot out of the very far corner.

Who owns that?

Don't know, Jackie Mac probably. I found it in the garage.

What are you doing with it?

Will you wait? Here, hold the torch for us.

She shoves her hand down into the welly and out come her secrets: first cigarettes and matches.

Are you *smoking*?

What do you think?

What about your asthma?

In the torchlight she sees Jeannie shrug.

She goes back to her secrets: next the scraps of paper that she writes her notes on.

I don't bother much with these anymore, she says. I just hide them here in case anyone finds them. And because Dad goes through the bin looking for Mam's bottles so they can have another row – God if you only saw him, rummaging through the bin like an oul tramp – I can't even throw them out.

She puts her hand back into the welly and out comes a large bar of chocolate.

Is that – ?

Here, Jeannie says, passing it over.

Oh thanks, I'm starved.

Anyway, never mind all that rubbish, *this* is what I really want to show you.

She plucks out a big lump of money.

I saved it out of the housekeeping. Loads isn't it? When the boot's all full to the top, then I'm running away. I won't be like Mam either, I'll last for more than two weeks. I'll last forever.

Tatty starts eating the chocolate.

While she's eating the chocolate she forgets about everything, all the things going on outside the alcove: Mam upstairs in her flat, Dad on his own in the bedroom downstairs. She forgets to be afraid about what's going to happen next. Because she's not on her own anymore, she's with Jeannie. Pals the two of them, for the first time ever – pals. Jeannie trusting her with all her secrets, talking to her without calling her names, making her feel sort of all grown up. And this mad happy feeling rushes right through her, the chocolate and Jeannie, the thrill of being grown up, the feel of the secret dark all around them.

Until Jeannie starts getting up off the cushion and says that it's time for bed.

Can we not stay here Jeannie, can we not just sleep here?

No. Tried it before. You wake up with cramps in your legs, a crick in your neck.

But where will I sleep?

In the end of the sofa.

Jeannie makes a bed on the sofa out of the winter coats. Tatty gets in in her uniform and tries to settle down. But her legs are too itchy from the wool of the coat on the wool of her tights. She takes off the tights. Her feet feel all clammy; she has a pain in her legs with the cold. So Jeannie makes a nest for her feet in the long nightie she wears over her clothes.

They talk into the dark.

How are the rows different now? Tatty asks.

Don't know, they just are.

Yeah but how?

Ah it's too hard to explain. They say things. Like what?

You know.

Do you mean like curses?

Yeah. And other things too.

You used to be always cursing – remember? Do you still curse now?

Sometimes. When I'm in the humour.

Dad called Mam this name in the car.

What name?

He said she was a cunt.

Yeah, I've heard that one before. That's nothing. It's the other things.

What things?

He says mad things to her, she says mad things back. Do you know what, I'm never drinking as long as I live.

Jeannie?

What?

I'm not either.

After a while Jeannie gets up and switches on the telly, keeping the sound turned right down, pushing the buttons into different stations till she finds the one that she wants. A man and a woman dancing and singing around a huge hotel room. There's a little fancy dog running around them. Tatty thinks the man's name might be Danny Kaye; she doesn't know the name of the woman nor the name of the fancy dog.

They watch for a few minutes and it all seems a bit stupid, watching without any sound. Until Jeannie starts playing this game. She turns Danny Kaye into Dad, the woman into Mam, giving them words to say like they do in their new sort of rows.

Tatty can't believe the sort of things Mam and Dad are saying to each other in the row. Some of the things she's heard before, but she never understood what they meant. Now she nearly understands. Even the things she never heard before make a new kind of sense that gives her such a fright she feels like crying. But she doesn't. She starts laughing instead. Jeannie is so funny, the way she can do the voices, the way she can fit all the words into their mouths at the exact right time.

And the man and the woman there on the telly twirling around, dancing away from each other then coming back again, with these mad smiles on their faces and their eyes all twinkly and their arms stretching in and out, saying those things to each other in their Mam and Dad voices.

They laugh so hard, they just can't stop. They laugh so hard Tatty has to sneak out to the toilet.

When she comes back into the living-room the telly is turned off, and the room is dark again.

She hears Jeannie's voice coming out from the end of the sofa.

I used to keep praying that the two of them would die. I used to pray they'd get in the car together and have a big crash. Then just die.

Don't say that Jeannie.

Well, I don't pray anymore.

What made you stop?

First because they're never in the car together anymore, second because there's no such thing as God. They just made him up.

She knows Jeannie is tired, can hear it in her voice, but she tries to keep her awake, telling her about Dad crashing the car, the skinny-malink woman, the man who turned out to be all right really in the end.

He even gave me a pound. You can have it for your welly if you like.

No, Jeannie mumbles, you keep it.

Do you want to hear what Laura's house was like? Tomorrow.

Then she tries asking Jeannie more questions, but Jeannie, so tired, only half-answers this time.

Hey Jeannie?

Huh?

Do you smoke here, in the house?

No. Only when I'm mitching.

You're *mitching*!

Mmm.

What's it like?

Crap.

Well who do you mitch with?

Meself.

Ah go on Jeannie, tell us.

Tomorrow, I'm tired.

Ah go on, now. Please.

Well … see after Dad kept me out of school for the two weeks, I didn't feel like …

What – you didn't feel like going back?

Mmm.

Where do you go?

Sometimes I just sit in churches, but …

But what?

The priest always ends up noticing you.

And what does he do? Does he throw you out?

No. Just might ask you what you're doing.

Is that all?

Annoying you as well. Asking do you want a chat or a cup of tea. So now mostly, you know …

What?
Walk.
Where?
Town.
Where in town?
Anywhere. Shhh.
What if you see someone you know?
I duck.
Where else do you go?
Once I went up to your school.
My school? How?
Got two buses, walked up the hill.
But why?
Don't know. Shhh.
What did you do when you got there?
Just looked.
What did you see?
Nothing. Shhh.
Jeannie – guess what?
What?
I'll be here for three weeks.
Huh?
Three weeks, that's how long I'll be here for the holidays.
I'll help you with everything. The dinner and everything.
Great. Shhh. Gotosleep.

She stays on her own then, facing the window, the stripy
light from the gaps in the venetian blinds, the bigger loop
of light in the middle where the blinds are broken down.
She thinks about Jeannie, trying to imagine what she's like
when she's mitching.

She sees Jeannie stuffing her school-bag in a bush somewhere, maybe the one where she used to throw all the Baby Power bottles a few years ago. She sees her hiding around the corner waiting on the bus to come along, putting out her hand then at the very last minute. Sneaking up the stairs, sitting in the back, her head turned away from the window. Then in town, wandering around, ducking in doorways if a policeman comes along or someone she thinks she might know. Counting the hours in the back of big churches, watching the jiggidy light from the candles, sitting on her feet, trying to keep them warm, and all the time listening for the sound of the priest's step coming.

Then she sees her standing outside her school in the middle of the trees all alone in the Phoenix Park. What would she see? Walls only, the windows in the top dorm maybe, the steeple of the school chapel, the top of a basketball hoop. All that way on two buses just to look at walls.

Then she thinks about Mam.

Mam. Asleep on her own in her makey-up flat, empty bottles under her bed. Two large, two medium, little baby ones. A family of bottles hiding under her bed.

The things Jeannie made her say in that horrible drunken voice that stopped being funny the minute Jeannie fell asleep.

She turns her head away from the window, into the back of the sofa. The taste of the chocolate still sweet in her mouth, the dry dusty taste of the sofa.

Three weeks is. Three sevens is. Twenty-one days.

1974

JACKIE MAC WAS THE ONE WHO DROVE HER BACK to school in the end, because Dad had to be someplace else. She was glad too, because, for the first time ever, she didn't want to be on her own with Dad, listening to him giving out stink about Mam, the way she used to have to listen to Mam giving out about him.

She thought she'd laugh out loud when the car finally drove through the gate. Thought she'd die of happiness at the sight of her school, the lights blasting out of all the windows, the driveway full of cars, of voices, of faces.

And all those lovely faces passing her in corridors and on the stairs as she hauled her case upwards, stopping to say hello, welcome back. And to listen to her lying through her teeth as well about what she got for Christmas, the brill time she'd had for the past three weeks and how, yes, it was just crap having to come back.

And her own bed waiting for her there against the wall, in her very own cubicle, everything just as she'd left it. She didn't even care anymore that her sheets were still dirty from three weeks ago because the washing-machine had been broken at home and she hadn't a clue how you go about sending stuff off to the Swastika laundry in Terenure.

She looked out the window and saw Laura's dad's car pulling up to the door. It would only be a few minutes before Laura would be here, Olivia too, probably full of their Christmas news, day by day, inch by inch. All of it true. Her own truth was starting to feel so heavy in her head, packed in tight like the stuff in her suitcase. She wished she could tell them, take everything out bit by bit. She wished she could tell them. But couldn't think how.

She thought about turning it into a story. A story all about this house on her road; two boys sitting up on the roof, drinking milk from bottles, throwing stones at the cars driving by. She could tell them about how this house drove the neighbours mad with its broken windows and the grass up sky high and the fights leaking out the walls every night. Or the spotty lounge boy that was sent to knock on its door on New Year's Eve in the late afternoon to collect the woman that lived there because the bar manager wouldn't serve her any more drink. She could tell them about the son and the daughter going down to the pub with the lounge boy not saying a word, walking a little bit ahead of them all the way. And the woman screaming at the barman outside the pub, You red-faced culchie, on the fiddle I bet. Get your fucking hands off me or I'll have you charged. She could tell them all about the girl and her brother trying to link the woman up the road, her swinging between them from side to side, the neighbours looking and hearing the boy tell his mother to fuck off, the mother so drunk she doesn't even notice, her mouth looking like it's hanging off her face, her handbag hanging open off her arm: lipstick, peppermints, cigarette lighter rolling all over the path. If she could just take a few things out of her head it would make it feel lighter. It wouldn't even have to be everything either. She needn't say who owned the house. She needn't say the woman was Mam.

But then the dorm-nun's hands came loudly clapping, up and down past all the cubicle rows, telling everyone they had to go back to their places and that meant Laura and Olivia only had enough time to pop their heads in for a second, say hello, give a quick wave.

She pulled the sheets out of her case real quick, made up the bed, got in in her dirty pyjamas. Stretching out slow, wiggling her toes, nuzzling her nose into the fleece of the candlewick spread, feeling all that space in the bed, all to her very own self. And the giddy sounds of the other girls in the dorm still unpacking their stuff and calling out to each other across the partitions. Happy and happy, never so happy.

Then out of nowhere she found herself crying.

The lights not even out yet, the Headgirl just starting the five-minute countdown. It gave her a right shock to hear herself crying. It gave everyone else a right shock too. Bit by bit, everything stopped. Even Rosemary's sniffling, her poor purple face popping over the partition.

Carrie? Carrie – is that *you*?

The dorm-nun looked strange sitting on the end of her bed a little while later when the lights were all out except for the night-light out in the corridor. Strange and small. She could have been one of the girls in her dressing gown and slippers, except for the white part of the veil still on her head, a tuft of dark hair sticking out under it.

The dorm-nun said nothing for ages; not about prayers nor about being brave; nothing at all until Tatty stopped crying.

Then she stood up, opened a big white hanky out and held it over Tatty's nose. Blow, she said.

Tatty blew, then the dorm-nun gave her the hanky for keeps.

I was down home myself this Christmas, the dormnun said. I know how hard it is to come back. Funny thing is, the nicer the Christmas, the harder it is to – would you not agree?

Tatty blew her nose again and said, Yes. Yes she would.

Cଧ

The teacher-nun gives them this vocabulary exercise. The exercise is a search for words. There's a prize for whoever does it the best.

Pick one word, the teacher-nun says, any one word at all, then what I want you to do is to write as many similar words as you can. For example: the word 'nice'. Think of all the words we know for 'nice'. There's lovely, and beautiful, and lots and lots of others. Different words that mean the same thing. But I want you to think of something other than 'nice', something a little more unusual. Use your imagination girls. Search inside your heads – you'll find words in there you didn't even know you had.

Tatty searches in her head for a suitable word. Tries the word 'cold', then the word 'hot'. Then the word 'big'. 'Small' after that.

She searches again and finds a different word. Tatty writes a heading at the top of the page. Then takes out her ruler underlining it neatly.

All The Words I Know For Drunk
Tipsy, twisted, merry, out of your tree, high as a kite.
Locked, legless, langer-oos, well on. Out of your
tiny mind. Mickey Monk, mouldy. Dipso, blotto.
Pissed, paralytic, plastered. Rotten. Stocious, steam-
ing. Buckled, bollixed. Flying, flutered, fucked.
Arseholes, alcoholic. Cunt.

She stares down at her list, and her eyes are burning. Then
she rips the page out, folds it up small and slips it into her
blouse pocket.

She opens a new page, presses it down, then goes back
to the word 'cold'.

○

Nothing for ages. Everything the same.

Then three weeks into term and the fourth day of
snow. She's called out of the ref, in the middle of breakfast
while it's still dark outside, with nearly a whole bowl of
cornflakes left and not even one sup taken out of her tea.
Everyone looking.

She crosses the ref, her face warm with shame, although
she can't think why or what for.

The little brown nun is waiting outside with her coat
and her scarf over her arms and she knows the minute she
sees her there that it's nothing she's done, something else
has to be wrong.

Sister?

The little brown nun doesn't answer, just takes her by
the hand and leads her through the school. They walk

down the corridors towards the senior school, past the back of the chapel and the chanting of nuns. They come out to the wide hall with the stairs up the middle. She notices she's taller than the little nun now.

They get to the main door and the nun helps her on with her coat, talking so softly to her she can hardly hear, has to lean her ear towards the little nun's mouth. She's not to worry, the little nun says. It's nothing serious, she's just needed at home.

But why Sister?

I really don't know.

She reaches up to Tatty, fixing a clip over the hole in her hair, then turns her around to check the plait at the back.

Perfetto, she says, and turns Tatty back around to face her. Then gives her a kiss on the forehead.

There's a taxi outside waiting. Go, go quick now go. You'll be back to us soon Cara. The sooner you go the sooner you'll return.

Tatty goes through the front hall door, stands on the steps for a second and knows in her heart that's not true. She can feel all the faces watching her through the frosty refectory windows, all the hundreds of eyes waiting for her to get into the taxi.

She opens the door, is about to get in when she hears the little brown nun calling to her. She turns around and the nun is running towards the taxi, dainty feet popping over the snow. One hand is holding her habit away from the snow, the other dangling a set of rosary beads. She presses the rosary into Tatty's hand.

Take care of these for me, Cara. Bring them back safe.

Tatty takes the beads and gets into the taxi, looks out the other window across white playing fields and a sky that is beginning to crack with light.

❧

No car in the driveway, just tracks from the tyres. The telephone is ringing as Luke answers the door. I thought you were Jeannie, he says, come back with the milk from the shop.

Why where's the milkman?

He doesn't come anymore.

She steps into the hall, looks up the stairs, sees the door of Mam's makey-up flat is wide-open. The telephone stops as she runs up the stairs: Mam's empty bed, the room in a mess. On the way back downstairs the telephone starts again. She knows that it has to be Dad. Listening for his voice behind the sounds of the phone: the tumble of coins, the clank of a thumped button A.

Dad, is that – ?

She can hear his breath like it's feeling around for words in the dark.

Dad? Daddy? Are you there? Is Mam with you? Send, his voice says.

Send? What do you mean? Send what Dad?

Send.

Oh Dad I don't even know what you're talking about. Why did you take me out of school? *Why?* And where's Mam?

The boys. Send the boys to school. The boys. And Deirdre. You and Jeannie stay home, mind Michael and clean up the mess.

Where's Mam?

Send the boys to school, and Deirdre. Mind Michael. You and Jeannie. Make sure the others are wrapped up well. And when you're cleaning up mind your hands – do you hear me now? I'd say that's an end to the snow, but make sure they're all wrapped up.

Is Mam – ?

Clean up. Wait there. That's all.

Dad? Dad? Are you there Dad?

She listens for a while in case he comes back.

The house is all grey and the house is all deaf because the snow won't let any noise get in. The light is too sharp and the light is too dull and that just drives her mad because it doesn't make sense the way it can be dull and be sharp all at once. But nothing about the snow makes sense to her now; the cold air that stands up on its own, waiting like a ghost every time you walk into a room. The innocent look of it out through the window, making you forget how much it's going to hurt you when it gets you outside, slapping the legs off you, cutting your face, stamping on your fingers, your toes. The way it tricks time into going so slow. And she thinks to herself, He's wrong about the snow, it can't be an end to it. Even if the snowflakes have stopped falling, or never fall again, it's still in charge of the day. She moves the handset away from and back into her ear.

Dad?

But there's only the long lonely belch of the telephone line.

She turns round and sees standing behind her Deirdre, Brian and Luke. Nobody speaks, not even Brian. Staring at the phone, staring at her, they move then, start looking for school things: lunches, bags, clothes for the snow.

The living-room floor: a crunch of glass under a boot. A crunch of glass again. Over by the fireplace a shorter sound, a crack – maybe a plate or a photo-frame. There's drawers to step over and drawers to step round. There's piles of papers that used to be stuffed in the drawers. A dining-room chair does a handstand in the corner; a bottle is toed and rolls over the lino, stops when it gets to the chair.

All eyes are avoiding the floor, to see just enough not to get cut.

All eyes except Deirdre's. Deirdre can't pretend not to see. Making her neck long so Tatty can wrap a scarf around it, holding her chin up for her hat to be tied, Tatty can feel her sister's fear in her hands.

Deirdre's feet shuffle and hop, her eyes fidget across the floor or dart down every few seconds to the space she stands in. It reminds Tatty of a horse, the way Deirdre keeps doing that. Afraid, as if the glass is alive, as if she thinks the glass is going to jump up and get her.

She takes Deirdre out into the hall where the floor is clear, then fattens her out with more heavy clothes. They squeeze in together on the bottom stair to wait for the special bus. Tatty puts her arms around the bulk of her big sister. Look at you, she says, all snuggy warm.

Nuggy, Deirdre repeats. Nuggywarm.

And she doesn't want Deirdre to go then, wants her to stay here instead, the two of them stuffed together on a stair, the warmth of Deirdre beside her.

You don't have to go Deedee, you can stay here with me and Jeannie and Michael, if you like.

Yeah. Where Mammy? Where her gone?

She'll be back in a little minute. You can stay here and I'll mind you, would you like that? We can make a snowman.

Yeah. A no-man!

The bus lights flicker into the hall and Deirdre jumps up.

Beep! she says. Beep mebus Tatty! Beep mebus! The bus horn sounds and Deirdre calls back to it, Beepbeepbeep!

Yes, Tatty says, opening the front door, beepyourbus. Hold on, hold on – what about me hug?

But Deirdre's bolted through the door.

Mind yourself Deirdre, don't fall – do you hear me? Mind yourself. Mind the snow.

From the doorstep she watches Deirdre waddle down the drive, pleased at the cuteness of her to stay in the tracks that Dad's car left behind.

Brian and Luke push out past her, start plodding through the thickest part of the snow to get to the gate.

What happened last night Brian? Luke?

Don't know, Luke says. Brian doesn't answer. He runs to the bus, starts rapping on its side, jumps up and down making faces at the special children inside.

Luke, barehanded, bareheaded, his coat swinging open stands on the kerb waiting, watching.

Luke? she calls out. Luke, come back. Your gloves, where's your hat?

He gets down off the kerb. Short run, long skid and he's on the other side of the road.

The bus moves off. She closes the door, sees the lights from Dad's car then filling up the hall.

Even in the new kitchen, he looks too big. The way he looks when he's driving a small car. His coat brushing off a towel on the back of a chair makes it fall on the floor. His heel presses down on a box of Rice Krispies that's lying in the jumble on the floor. You can't see his eyes under his hat but you can see his chin is crispy and black. The top of his pyjamas is sticking out over his jumper; the bottoms of his pyjamas are sticking out of the end of the trousers.

It takes her a few seconds to notice that Jeannie has come in and is standing behind him in the doorway, a bottle of milk held in each hand.

Where's Mam? Tatty asks.

He opens the press under the sink and pulls out a bottle of brandy, then starts flipping the doors of presses open looking for a glass.

Fuckit, he says, taking a cup off the draining board.

The brandy gurgles into the cup and the kitchen fills up with the smell of Christmas.

Dad please – where is she?

He rubs his chin for a minute. In hospital, he says.

Why? What's wrong with her? Answer me Dad. Jeannie?

She wrecked the place, Jeannie says, then tried to kill herself.

That's right, Dad says. She wrecked the place. Then tried to kill herself. And do you know why? Do you know why? Because you lot drove her to it.

Us lot? Jeannie goes, making a space for the milk on the table. *Us?*

Between your mitching and the rest of the carry-on it's no wonder, and let me tell you this, if she dies, if she –

It is *not* our fault, Tatty says. It is not.

What she has to put up with from you lot, what she –

I don't even live here Dad. I don't even live in this house.

Ask her. Ask her about her mitching, he says, pointing at Jeannie.

Tatty can hear herself screaming.

Just a scream on its own for a minute, then words and a scream together. It's not our fault Dad. It's yours. YOUR fault. YOURS. It's *all* your fault.

He stays still for minute, then puts his hand in his pocket and pulls out a roll of money. Twice he flicks his thumb off his tongue, then slaps two notes on the table. For messages, he says.

He drinks the brandy, puts the cup in the sink, then walks to the door.

He stands in the doorway, looking at them both, looking at the kitchen.

I'm – he says. I'm –

But he doesn't say what he is.

She thinks he might be crying. She wants to run out after him and give him a hug but she's afraid to touch him now. And anyway she has so much to do. Finish cleaning the kitchen. Then the living-room: pick up the bottles, the broken ornaments, the dress-dance photograph with the crack in the middle. And then Michael's breakfast – she was nearly forgetting about Michael's breakfast and Michael's nappy that will have to be changed and ...

She feels her hands hopping under the teacloth, the plate trying its best to slip out of her hands. That would mean *more* broken things on the floor. She puts the plate down and stands in the middle of the floor.

Jeannie puts on the kettle. Ask Alice, she whispers. Alice will know.

CR

Alice gives her this hug at the door, and that makes her think that it must be true about Mam. Then she brings her into the room that's called the breakfast-room in Alice's house.

Alice puts a soft yellow jumper around her shoulders, makes her sit at the fire, drink hot sugary tea, eat thick marmalade on toast.

My Mam tried to kill herself, she tells Alice. She might be going to die.

Oh no darling, she's not going to die. Where in the name of God did you get that idea?

Dad said. He said it was all our faults.

Whose fault?

Us. For being so bold and Jeannie for mitching school.

Alice kneels down beside her chair and takes a hold of her arms. And her face doesn't look like Alice's face, her skin too pale, her eyes sort of baldy, her lips too small when she speaks.

Listen to me now Caroline. Your Mam isn't going to die. She didn't try to kill herself at all.

But why is she in hospital then?

She just took too many sleeping tablets by mistake, love, that's all.

By mistake?

Yes. It was an accident. Who's at home now?

Jeannie and Michael. Dad, maybe. But he might be gone out by now.

Look, Alice says, why don't I get dressed and then I'll drive you home? Finish your toast, there's a good girl. Take more tea there. I'll be back in a jiffy.

It's warm in Alice's house, in her lovely breakfast-room with fruit in a bowl on a shiny table, a dark red carpet on the floor. And the sounds are nice too: a man on the radio telling jokes, the washing-machine in the room next door that's called a utility-room in Alice's house. Even out the back looks nice through the window. A slide and a see-saw, a neat wooden shed at the wall, a snowman turning brown at the edges like a fruit going off. She wants to stay here, with Alice's soft jumper keeping her warm.

Alice comes back with her face coloured in and she looks like Alice again.

If Dad knows it was an accident. I mean if he *knows*. Then why? Why did he say – ?

He's just upset love, that's all. Has to blame someone. He always has to have someone to blame. You know yourself what he's like.

Tatty says oh yes, she knows what he's like. But when she thinks about it, she doesn't.

ॐ

Mam comes home a few days later and she's shaky and white from taking her too many tablets by mistake.

Or trying to kill herself you mean, Jeannie keeps saying.

Dad walks her softly into the living-room, one arm around her, the other arm for carrying her suitcase. Look who's home! he says with a big Danny Kaye smile on his face. Look who I have here!

Deirdre runs to give Mam a hug; Brian and Luke step near her, then stop; Michael hides behind Jeannie and peeps out all shy. Tatty stays by the wall and waits to hear if Mam will tell them all her story about where she's been and why. Then she remembers that Mam doesn't explain herself. I don't have to explain myself to you, is what Mam always says. I don't have to explain myself to *anybody*.

Then Dad tells them to turn off the telly and say hello to Mam.

Mam says hello back and that they're all looking well and that they have the place lovely and clean. You can barely hear what she's saying. So even if she did want to tell them all her story about where she's been or why, you probably wouldn't be able to hear, her voice is that quiet.

Then she says she's a bit tired.

So Dad takes her into bed. Not up to her makey-up flat, but to her old room where she used to sleep before.

He comes out a few minutes later and says that he wants to have a little chat. Then tells them to sit on the sofa.

Your Mam has been very sick, he says, but she's going to get well again. We'll all have to help her though. Be very, very good. No fighting, no shouting – do you hear me now Buster? he says to Brian. No messin'. And no more mitching either Missy, he halfwinks at Jeannie.

I know things haven't been great, but everything's going to change from now on. Everything's going to be different. I'm getting the house all fixed up – you won't believe it when you see it, the nicest house on the road, it'll be. We'll wear that Jackie Mac fella out with work. And as for the neighbours? The neighbours won't know what hit them. I'm even thinking of getting a coloured telly for Mam! Because guess what? Mam has stopped drinking. So. A whole new start. No more drinking from Mam. No more rows. And here's the best news of all – no more Tatty living away from her family: she's going to stay home in future. With us. Where she belongs. Won't that be great Tatty?

Yes Dad.

Everything is going to change from now on, he says again. Everything's going to be different.

Then he tells them he has to go out for a while to see a man about a bit of business and they're not to make any noise so Mam can have a big fat sleep for herself.

The switched off telly is dark and green; it holds a dark-green picture of the living-room on its screen. The screen is curved and bends everything into a funny shape. But you'd still know it was the living-room. The sideboard at the back wall, the corner of an armchair, a bit of the window, the sofa at the front.

Tatty looks into the screen. She sees the shapes of her brothers and sisters squeezed in together on the sofa.

She sees Jeannie's long curly hair and Brian's football cap.

She sees Luke trying to get a suck off his thumb on the sly.

She sees Deirdre's head bent forward studying her shoes.

She sees Michael rubbing his ear with his fist.

She sees everyone except for herself.

Tatty can't see her own face, only a pair of hands that must be hers joined together around Michael to hold him steady on her knee.

It's like a small dark photograph deep in the centre of the screen.

It's like they're sitting there watching themselves on the telly.

Questions for the Reader

1. The narrator of *Tatty* is a child. How well do you think this works? Did it ring true?
2. How effective was the child's voice in telling the story of her parents – should they have been given their own voices?
3. What was your first reaction to this book – did it draw you in at once or did it take a while to become accustomed to the unusual tone?
4. How well do you think it dealt with the subject of alcoholism and its effect on the family unit?
5. Did it make you think about women's lives in the 1960s and 1970s and how much has changed in this regard?
6. Did the structure of the book work for you?
7. Tatty has a sister with special needs. How do you think this affected the family? And how well did the author deal with this situation?
8. Which character did you relate to most and what do you think connected you to him or her?
9. If you could hear the story from another character's point of view, who would that be?
10. What did you think of the length of the book? Was it too short or did it end in the right place? Did you like the ending?
11. How well did you think the author captured Dublin in the 1960s and 1970s?

12. Have you read any other books with a similar subject matter, for example, the effect of alcoholism on a family or living with a child with special needs?
13. What do you think happened to the family after the novel ended?
14. Have you read any other books by this author and if so, are there any similarities?
15. If you could ask the author one question, what would it be?